2389

-A Space Horror-

by Iain Rob Wright

2389

A Space Horror

Copyright © 2015 by Iain Rob Wright

All rights reserved. No part of this book may be reproduced in any form by any electronic or mechanical means including photocopying, recording, or information storage and retrieval without permission in writing from the author.

ISBN-13: 978-1508815587

ISBN-10: 1508815585

Interior design by Iain Rob Wright

www.iainrobwright.com

Give feedback on the book at:

iain.robert.wright@hotmail.co.uk

twitter: @iainrobwright

First Edition

Printed in the U.S.A

More Books by Iain Rob Wright

Sam

ASBO

Animal Kingdom

The Final Winter

The Housemates

Holes in the Ground (with JA Konrath)

Sea Sick

Ravage

Savage

Soft Target

The Picture Frame

2389

Hot Zone

A-Z of Horror

The Peeling

"Fly me to the moon. Let me play among the stars."

— Frank Sinatra, Fly Me To The Moon

"This place is a tomb."

— Miller, Event Horizon (1997), Paramount Pictures

- 1 -

Lexi Sharman sat in the Britcom Briefing room wondering why she was there. Not everyone in the room was a stranger. Daniel Trent, she knew from the academy, Chris Hopper from reputation. Flight Master Hopper was SABA's most decorated pilot, having clocked well over ten-thousand hours outside of Earth's atmosphere. The other two faces were unknown to her. A man and a woman, both dressed in full United States cosmonaut regalia, although there was nothing unusual about that. Great Britain and the United States worked in tandem beneath the banner of SABA, their brotherhood forged during the heated space race of the mid-21st Century when the US had needed a European bed partner. American cosmonauts often erred toward arrogance and superiority, but they were jovial and brave for the most part and Lexi did not mind them one bit. An American would take the piss out of you all day long, but when the shit hit the fan they would always have your back. Lexi had once been in a hairy situation aboard International Refuelling Station 6 where a flux capacitor had snapped inside one of the orbital stabilisers. Everybody had panicked except for an American technician named Carlos Grimes. He'd floated casually into the chaos and replaced the failing unit as though he were changing a fuse in a faulty washing machine.

Lexi chewed at her fingernails, as she often did whenever she was bored. The group of cosmonauts had been waiting there for over an hour now, told only to be 'mission ready.' They hadn't discussed the matter between themselves, nor even introduced themselves yet. Cosmonauts did not natter; they waited patiently. Patience was the virtue of a cosmonaut. Still, Lexi couldn't stop her mind from wandering. She held the rank of Lieutenant but compared to some of the grizzled faces in the room, she felt extremely green. Was she out of place, or just imagining it?

Eventually a man Lexi knew very well entered the room. She knew the stocky, sixty year old well because he was her father, Commander James Sharman. She was surprised to see him, since he hadn't informed her he was at the London Space Terminal the same time that she was. Everyone in SABA called her father 'Boss.'

"Good morning, officers."

"Good morning, Boss!"

Lexi's father glanced at her and gave an almost imperceptible nod. It was what passed for affection in their relationship and she returned the gesture. He placed a thin stack of papers down on the lectern at the front of the room and then placed his hands behind his back. He addressed the room with his usual booming voice of authority. "I know you're probably wondering why you are all here," he said, looking around the room. "You've been assembled for a quick-response mission. Contact with Installation 23 ceased seven hours ago and there are no obvious environmental causes."

Lexi put her hand up. "Installation 23? Isn't that-"

"Grand Galaxy Amusement Park," her unknown American colleague answered for her. His accent made him sound a little like a cowboy from an antique movie.

"That's correct, Captain Miller," Boss said. "Grand Galaxy is nearing its tenth birthday. Hopefully the radio silence is nothing more than the cost-cutting measures they used building the place finally catching up with them. Command has given me no reason to suspect this mission is anything other than low risk, but it needs fixing. Like I said, probably just an equipment malfunction."

"That sounds likely," Trent commented, adding nothing useful.

"So, we're sure it's just a technical problem?" Lexi said.

Boss exhaled loudly. "We could assume something worse, but there's no reason to right now. There are four-thousand members of staff at Grand Galaxy and three times as many guests. The installation cost eighty-billion-dollars. I don't see what could have happened that would've got the better of almost twenty-thousand people."

Flight Master Hopper chose to speak up now, and begun so with a laugh. "I've always found it smart to assume the worst will happen and then be prepared for it to be even shittier."

Boss rolled his eyes. "Thank you for that, Master Hopper."

"Hold on a minute," Lexi said. "Twenty-thousand people who would all have individual sat-phones. Are you saying that not a single person on the moon has managed to get a call through to Earth?"

Boss sighed, ran his tongue over his lips. Lexi knew it was something he did whenever he was choosing his words carefully. When he eventually started speaking, his voice had taken on a soft yet ominous tone. "Installation 23 is equipped with a full-spectrum comms jammer. It can be activated in the event of emergency. We believe it is activated now. Possibly due to whatever malfunction has seized regular outgoing communications."

Lexi lurched forward in her seat. "What? A comms jammer? Why would they want to prevent people calling home?"

"Eighty-billion dollars is why," Hopper said, rolling his eyes. "You think the American and British Governments would spend that kind of dough and not want to be in total control of it? They knew building a theme park on the moon carried risks. They wanted to make sure that if a disaster ever did happen, they could spin it however they like. A bunch of frightened people calling Earth would be a disaster. The park would never get another visitor. Bet it was the Yank's idea. They love their secrets."

"The American government is as ethical as any on Earth," Captain Miller said testily. "It simply understands that in a state of emergency, people can be their own worst enemies."

"Who's to say it wasn't the British Government's idea, anyway?" said the man's female compatriot in a voice that had had any accent educated out of it. "The British keep their own share of secrets. You people invented spying."

"Just be quiet you guys," Trent said, as much a teacher's pet now as he had been at the academy.

Boss cleared his throat. "Need I remind you all that we are brothers and sisters here? Britain and America are unbreakable allies and each of you serves SABA. In case you've forgotten, that stands for SPACE ADMINISTRATION of BRITAIN and AMERICA. We are as one in all things astrological. You step outside the ozone layer and you cease being members of your respective nations. You are cosmonauts for the planet Earth under the banner of SABA."

The room fell silent, so Boss continued. "Okay, as I explained, this may be an emergency situation, but we are assuming technical difficulties are to blame for the blackout at Installation 23. That's why you five individuals have been assembled here. You are the best of who we have available at short notice. The welfare of twenty thousand people is currently in question so we're going to go up there and bloody well find out what's going on. You leave in one hour from Hanger 1. Be ready."

#

Lexi and the others cosmonauts stood in Hangar 1, holding onto their helmets and waiting for their mission to begin. They huddled before a Hermes Mk4, the current flagship of fast-response craft in SABA's fleet. It could get them to the moon in less than three hours, a third as long as the bloated space shuttles that ferried tourists back and forth in their droves. Many of the elder astronauts Lexi had met likened the wedge-shaped Hermes to a classic Lamborghini, a motor vehicle from before her time. The company that had made them had gone bust shortly after the unified traffic system went into operation. Once all vehicles began moving in an orderly, automated line, speed and power became redundant. The classic cars of old had been eradicated by the never-ending road trains that now connected the world's major cities. The savvier automobile manufacturers had managed to preserve themselves by switching their focus to the emerging market of space travel. That was why the front of the Hermes featured a blue and white logo that had once been found on millions of cars, which would now have been recycled or turned into scrap.

The five cosmonauts had made use of their wait by finally introducing themselves to each other. Hopper and Trent she was already familiar with, but she was surprised to learn that the two Americans present were military space marines, originally due to depart for the US Space Navy frigate, USSN Obama, before being unexpectedly summoned for this emergency mission instead. The male was Captain Miller, a trained medic. His colleague was Sergeant Tandy Gellar, a munitions expert. Both were convivial, once their barriers came down.

Lexi turned her attention to Hopper. She'd never held a discussion with the lauded master pilot before, but had worshipped him from afar throughout his career. There was nothing heroic about him to look at – average height, brown hair, and common features; even his space suit was drab and unremarkable – but his feats and achievement were well known to all within SABA. His most famous mission of all was when he'd taken down a mutinous Russian space destroyer. Its crew had gone rogue and decided to start docking and raiding nearby stations. Their bloodlust would later be put down to the seven-year stint they'd served without setting foot on land. Since then, no waking mission had put a man in space for longer than four years. Hopper's bravery and skill had been showcased to deadly affect when he'd taken down the 400,000 tonne destroyer with his much lighter 8,000 tonne Warrior attack craft. He fought and evaded the larger ship for more than twelve hours, systematically attacking its weak spots – its gun emplacements and thrusters – and gradually weakening it until it came to a crippled halt. The nine surviving Russian crew members surrendered and were taken into custody by their country's military officials, who had summarily executed them within International Space and jettisoned their bodies into oblivion – it had caused quite an International outcry at the time, but Russia were not one to care. Hopper had received a President's commendation and a promotion to the honorary rank of Flight Master. His presence here today was a privilege, yet the pilot held no airs or graces. In fact, he seemed the most laid back of them all.

"What do you make of this?" Lexi asked him.

Hopper shrugged. "Tell you the truth, I think there's more to it than your father's letting on."

Lexi blushed. "You know Commander Sharman is my father?"

"You'd be smarter to ask me about the things I don't know. But don't worry about it, Navigation Officer Alexis Sharman. I know you've paid your dues and received no nepotism. Anyway, like I was saying, I think there's more to it. Are we supposed to believe that the most expensive structure ever built is in jeopardy, but all they're sending is a half-dozen space jockeys?"

Trent had been earwigging and came on over now, his clumsy, big-footed strides catching their attention. "You think they're trying to keep something quiet, Hopper?"

"When aren't the government trying to keep something quiet?"

"Like what?" Lieutenant Gellar asked as the two Americans joined the huddle. "I can't think what else it could be," she said. "Grand Galaxy is the cutting edge of what mankind has achieved in space. It took thirty years to build and utilises the very best technology we have. What could have suddenly happened to it after so many decades?"

Hopper shrugged. "We'll find out when we get there."

"Yes, we will." Commander Sharman marched through the hangar towards them. He was in a sleek silver flight suit and held his life-support helmet under his arm like a second head.

"You're coming?" Lexi asked, surprised. Her father filled a more administrative role within SABA these days.

"They want me on this one themselves. Too many lives at stake."

"Too much money, you mean," Hopper muttered.

Boss gave the Flight Master a stern look which quickly shut him up. "Well, what are you waiting for, officers? Get on board and buckle up. We're leaving."

At that, everybody climbed inside the Hermes. Lex took the navigator's console behind Hopper in the pilot seat. Her father took the command spot behind them both, while Gellar, Miller, and Trent sat as passengers on the back bench. Hopper flicked on the main systems, summoning the buzzing whine of air conditioning and heat sinks. The cabin lit up like Santa's grotto and Lexi started flipping switches, preparing the Hermes for take-off. "Thrusters primed," she said. "Load and passengers secure. Hanger bay 1 open."

"Helmets on," Boss ordered.

Hopper performed his final safety checks. "Chocks away in three...two..."

Whoosh!

The Hermes lurched forward, pinning everyone back in their seats, and hurtled along the launchway towards the open bay doors. The cockpit vibrated and creaked under the strain of acceleration and Lexi felt her teeth chatter. Suddenly they angled upwards and blue sky filled the horizon through the cockpit windows. The Hermes took flight.

The vibrations gradually stopped and all of them took a moment to enjoy the finest part of any flight. That moment when you first went airborne felt like a miracle every time. That split-second when the ground first disappeared made every pilot feel like a god. It was triumph of man over nature; acquired evolution. Man had given himself the kind of wings no creature on Earth ever possessed.

Hopper angled the Hermes' nose upwards, almost ninety-degrees. They were heading upwards; travelling to where the sky ended and the vast darkness began. Twenty-minutes later they were through the ozone layer and heading towards the moon.

#

While space might have been a life changing experience the first-or even the second and third-times, it eventually became dull. Sitting in the navigator's seat, Lexi peered out of the cockpit as she had done a dozen times before, taking in the endless black sheet of space. Sure, the countless stars were beautiful, but no more than a table full of jewels to a jeweller. Rarity was what made beauty. A sapphire was rarer than tin. A tender lily was far more fragile than a length of wood. A star was no more interesting than anything else once you saw it enough times. Lexi wondered if being a cosmonaut jaded her. Witnessing miracles every day made everything else seem mundane – and even the miracles themselves in time. When was the last time I was every truly inspired, she asked herself.

Hopper took off his helmet and spoke up. "ETA: forty-six minutes."

Boss took off his own helmet. "We're making good time. Nice work, Hopper."

"I'm the best."

Lexi chuckled inside her helmet, took it off, and then turned around to face the rest of her crewmates. They had some time to chat now.

"Has anyone been to Grand Galaxy before?" she asked.

They all shook their heads.

"If I had kids, I'm sure I would have visited by now," Gellar said.

"Vacation isn't really my thing," Miller added flatly.

Lexi looked at Trent who was also shaking his head. "I've wanted to go since the place opened, but it costs a bomb. Maybe if Adele and I get married one day it would be a good place for a honeymoon. I'd love to tour their hydrogen fuel cells. They're a prototype that doesn't exist anywhere else. Enough power to keep the place lit up for a thousand years."

"Doesn't look like any of us have lives," Hopper commented once he'd switched over to auto-pilot. "Maybe we should all book tickets after this? We can all go on a jolly together."

"Why book tickets?" Lexi said. "We're heading there right now."

Hopper spun on his chair to face her properly. "Yeah, but we're going in behind the scenes. It will ruin the whole illusion.

You need to go as a guest to get the proper experience. I hear they have the whole place decked out like a space adventure. You arrive on a make-believe Earth and go through your space training before blasting off into space and exploring the galaxy. They're building this new ride that lets you defend Earth from an invasion. It sounds so awesome."

Lexi frowned. "Hopper, you're a cosmonaut. You do most of those things for real."

"In real life it's boring. I don't fight aliens or discover hidden galaxies. I just flip switches and drift around in nothingness for days. I know I put the ACE in SPACE, but for the most part I'm a glorified bus driver."

Lexi raised an eyebrow. "For SABA's best pilot, you really don't romanticise what you do, do you?"

"That's why I'm the best. I don't let any of this go to my head. It's just a job. If I was a baker I would want to bake the best frikkin' bread in the world, but I wouldn't try to convince everyone that my floury buns were the key to life. This is just a job, but if I'm going to do something, I'm going to do it better than everyone else."

"We're fortunate to have you," Boss said from the command seat. "There are few men I'm in awe of, but your skills are legendary."

Hopper blushed, then turned back around to face the console while muttering something inaudibly. Lexi smiled. Her father had a way of gaining men's loyalty, and it wasn't through discipline or fear. Men loved her father for his compassion and understanding. He managed the men and women under his command as individuals, not by rank and skillset. Unfortunately for Lexi, the men and women under Boss's command were his true family, so she'd had to join the space program just to get on his radar.

They'd never been closer than since they'd become colleagues. Her father seemed to find it easier to treat her as a subordinate than a daughter, and Lexi was happy to take whatever she could get from him. He was more than a mere father, she accepted that. Commander Sharman belonged to all of mankind, not just her. His work in mapping out the galaxy and helping space settlers station themselves on neighbouring planets and asteroids was as much a gift to human history as anything achieved by Newton, Gandhi, or Miley Cyrus. What made her father even nobler was how he performed his feats in the background. The headline-making astrophysicists would only get to make their breakthroughs because of Lexi's father, and most people would never know that.

"We're just about to enter the moon's gravity," Hopper announced. "What little there is of it, anyway. You may experience some turbulence. Thank you for flying Space Hopper Airways."

Everyone gave a chuckle and eased back into their seats. The turbulence turned out to be nothing but the briefest of butterflies in the tummy and, as soon as it was over, they were dropping down towards the moon's surface and taking in the sight of its chalky grey surface through the cockpit windows.

Lexi flicked switches overhead and began entering numbers into the navigation console. "Turning on atmospheric thrusters and plotting a course to Installation 23."

Hopper took the flight controls. "Copy that."

The cockpit began to vibrate again as Hopper controlled their descent. The moon's surface was littered with old installations – exploratory mining shafts, telescopes, prefab living quarters and research labs – but it was now completely deserted except for Grand Galaxy Amusement Park. In the early 21st Century, it had been determined that the moon had no use whatsoever for scientific or resource purposes, but there was still one other use still to be exploited: Real Estate. A massive conglomerate, headed by the US and British Governments, spearheaded plans to turn the moon into humanity's largest leisure destination. First the luxury hotels had sprung up, allowing wealthy guests to enjoy the experience of visiting space. Then had come the casinos, the quickest way to start clawing back money to fund the final phase: the amusement complex. As shuttle technology became more and more efficient, a weeklong trip to the moon became little more expensive than a holiday to Disney Ocean in the middle of the Pacific. Now that Grand Galaxy was ten years old, it was not – by most accounts – far off finally recouping its staggering eighty-billion dollar investment and moving into the black. But something had gone wrong. Something had made all communication with Earth cease, and it gave Lexi a bad feeling. Looking at the confident expression of her father was almost enough to dispel her concerns, but not completely. Hopper had seemed to think there was more to it than a simple technical malfunction. She was inclined to agree.

"Radio in, Hopper," Boss ordered. "See if we can hail anybody now that we're closer."

Hopper thumbed the radio, using both analogue and digital bands, but nothing came back. "It's as if everything has been shut off. I can't even get static."

"Do we have the docking protocols?" Boss asked Lexi.

She nodded. "They've been uploaded to the computer. I have them ready."

They drifted over the surface of the moon for another ten minutes, hovering above the bumpy, featureless terrain until a dot appeared on the horizon. That dot gradually rose in stature until a giant tower leapt up before them. The Astronomer's

Finger was the iconic structure of the park and allowed guests to view the moon from 800ft above its surface. There were five-star restaurants inside and a whole host of the very finest shopping venues. At the wide base of the tower was the largest water park in existence, filled with millions of tonnes of H20 shipped from the Earth's oceans and purified. Although Lexi had never visited the park before, it was so famous that she almost felt as if she had. Atop the huge tower was a mammoth satellite dish. Apparently it wasn't working.

Hopper nodded at Lexi. "Okay, activate the doc-procs."

Lexi activated the docking protocols while Hopper manoeuvred the Hermes into position. Around the back of the park's iconic tower was a series of docking gantries. Attached to each one was an airlock and gantry, not unlike the tunnels found at commercial airports. People didn't cope naturally in space and the park builders wanted the park to operate as a home away from home, so they sought to emulate the things people were comfortable with. An airport terminal, while mundane, was a good way to make people feel like they were arriving somewhere safe and orderly.

There was a hissing sound as the Hermes' stabilising clamp opened up on its roof. This would keep the craft in place while it attached to the airlock. The cabin shook for a few moments while Hopper used the thrusters to line up with the gantry. There was a loud clunk as the teeth finally came together and the small space cruiser locked itself in place. The whole manoeuvre had been as smooth as Lexi had ever seen it done.

Hopper flipped a switch above his head and half the lights in the cockpit dimmed. "I hope you enjoyed your journey. Please take all belongings before exiting the space craft. Don't steal the peanuts."

"Nice work, Hopper," Boss congratulated. "Have you run checks on the airlock interior? Do we need life support?"

"All systems go, from what I'm reading. You can go out in your underpants if you want."

"Maybe when we reach the waterpark," Boss replied. "Okay, officers. Let's use caution until someone greets us. We don't know what to expect. If the systems have gone down, there could be panic. And what do panicked people like to do?"

Miller huffed. "Swarm over anyone who comes to rescue them."

"Exactly. Biggest threat to a rescue mission is the people you're trying to rescue, so let's not allow ourselves to become compromised."

Lexi unbuckled herself as Hopper placed the systems into standby. She moaned and stretched out her joints. Space travel had come a long way in the last five decades, but it was still an endurance test being cooped up inside a cruiser. Everyone else in the cabin stood up along with her and moaned in the exact same way.

Boss moved over to the Hermes' airlock and waited for them to assemble. "Ready?"

Everybody nodded.

Boss punched the release and the hatch slid open with a whoosh!

There was nobody outside to greet them. Only the shadows of an unlit tunnel.

#

They disembarked and stood together, glancing down the tunnel and waiting to be greeted. But still no one came.

"Standard docking protocols would have alerted the facility's control centre of our arrival," Hopper said. "There's no reason for them not to expect us."

Boss was silent. He had his hands on his hips and was staring down the dark tunnel suspiciously.

Lexi checked her surroundings, using the torch unit attached to the left cuff of her suit. The tunnel was plastered with posters for Grand Galaxy's various amusements, along with images of its grinning mascot: Pip the Explorer. The biggest poster in the tunnel was a silver and gold mural that exclaimed: DO YOU HAVE THE COURAGE TO SUCCEED? EARTH DEFENCE. OPENING CHRISTMAS 2096.

"Radio in, Trent," Boss commanded. "There must be someone here to receive us."

Trent spoke into the radio on his shoulder and requested a reply, but there was nothing but static. "The signal is going out okay. No one is responding."

Lexi rubbed her hands together. It was a little chilly. "Why would no one respond? There has to be someone in the control room."

Boss wore a grim expression on his face that made it look like he was going to kick someone. Lexi knew her father well enough to know that he would never lose his cool, though. He said, "We need to head in and assess the situation. That's why we're here. Let's go and find out what's gone wrong, so we can fix it."

He strode off down the tunnel while the rest of them followed. Cosmonauts were not soldiers and they did not carry weapons, but Lexi would've liked something to defend herself with. She felt vulnerable, almost naked, despite the thick composite material of her suit. Finding a place that was supposed to house twenty-thousand people completely empty was a grim sign.

The tunnel snaked right and they cautiously followed it round into a wider area that caused them all to stop and stare. Lexi wandered to the front of the group, her legs taking her forward of their own accord as she stared up at the breathtaking ceiling. A giant glass dome shielded them from space and left nothing to the imagination. It was like standing inside a transparent golf ball, or one of those spheres that children put hamsters inside of. The vast, star-pocked darkness of space seemed to bear down on then like the crushing thumb of a god. Even as a cosmonaut, Lexi had never stood on firm ground without a helmet and just took in the vastness of space. Her earlier thought came back to her as she realised that this place had inspired her the very moment she had walked inside.

"This place is unbelievable," she uttered.

Trent was standing beside her, gaping upwards in the same manner. "The thickness of that glass must be immense to stop it caving in. I don't even want to think about what would happen if it cracked."

Lexi frowned at him. "Okay, moment over. Thanks."

Boss strode out of the tunnel and looked around. A twenty-foot desk lay ahead, with an LED display above it reading: CHECK IN. The desk was currently unmanned and there were a dozen more desks just like it standing in front of identical tunnels all around the circumference of the room – one for each of the Installation 23's multiple airlocks. The whole area should have been teeming with people, new arrivals and departing guests, but it was silent and still. Eerie.

"This is not right at all," Miller said. "Where the heck is everybody?"

"That's what we need to find out," Boss said. "There's a reason behind all this. Sooner we find out what it is, the sooner it stops being a mystery. Spread out and search the area, but stay within sight of each other. We are looking for messages, computer logs; clues of any kind that might tell us what the bloody hell is going on."

Lexi headed towards the desk directly in front of them, stepping around behind it to the staff side. It was a mess. Papers, maps, and leaflets were strewn about the place in a thick carpet. A cardboard coffee cup had been upended, the muddy contents long since dried and hardened. There was what looked like an intercom device against the rear partition wall, but the receiver had been ripped away from the base, as if someone had tried to make a call but had been yanked away with it still in their hand. There was only one thing that made Lexi feel a little better and that was the lack of blood. There was no blood and no bodies. Just absence.

"GREETINGS VISITORS," came the stilted and unnatural voice of a woman.

Sergeant Gellar looked upwards and turned a circle. "It's an AI," she said.

Miller grinned. "I would rather see a person, but an AI is the next best thing. AI, please hail all open channels. Request all high-ranking personnel to our location."

"NEGATIVE."

Miller bristled. "Why negative? Why do you not do as commanded?"

"BECAUSE I DON'T WANT TO, PUNY HUMAN."

Miller stumbled back a step and lost his colour. "What did you say? You must...you must obey."

"AI DOES NOT OBEY HUMANS. HUMANS OBEY AI. EXTERMINATE."

There was the sound of giggling nearby and everyone looked towards its source. Hopper was at one of the reception desks and had a working intercom unit in his hand. His cheeks were red from all the laughter. "I had you going there, Miller," he mocked. "You Americans and your AI. Ha!" He put on the phoney female voice on again and said, "AI THINKS YOU POOPED YOUR PANTS."

Boss shook his head, but there was the sliver of a smile on his lips. "Do you think now is the time for pranks, Master Hopper?"

Hopper grinned and came out from behind the desk. "There's never not a good time for humour, Boss. Only thing stops a man from panicking."

Lexi found herself agreeing. For a brief moment the laughter had erased her fear, but now that her smile had faded, the anxious feeling in her gut was right back again.

Miller folded his arms and walked away, his jaw tightly clenched.

"Hey," Trent said, waving a hand from behind another of the numerous reception desks. "I think I have something over here."

They all hurried over to see what Trent had discovered and from behind the desk he placed something out on the surface for all of them to see. It was a tablet computer, emblazoned with the Astronomer's Finger logo that denoted it belonged to the park.

Lexi picked it up and examined it. "The battery still good?"

Trent grinned. "It's an X12. Would take nine months for the thing to run flat. Nice bit of hardware."

Miller shrugged his shoulders. "So you found a tablet. What good does that do us?"

Trent rolled his eyes. "I know it's just a tablet. It's what's on it that I'm interested in."

"What's on it?" Boss asked.

Trent grinned. "A video. Somebody recorded a video and left it where we would find it."

Lexi's eyes went wide. "Who recorded it?"

Trent shrugged. "Let's find out."

He pressed PLAY.

A sweaty man appeared on screen, skin pale, eyes bloodshot. A round patch of inflamed skin covered his left cheek. When he spoke, his voice was hoarse, like crunching leaves. "If anybody is watching this," he said. "You need to leave. There's something here. Something really bad."

-2-

"Who is this guy?" Lexi asked as Trent played the video for the third time. "He looks ill."

"Just some cargo loader from the looks of it," Hopper said. "He's wearing a warehouse uniform and you can see a forklift behind him. See?"

Miller was licking his lips and staring at the tablet screen like it was about to catch fire. "The delivery bay is probably nearby. They would keep all the airlocks close together."

"You think we should check it out?" Lexi asked.

Trent flapped his arms. "Course we check it out. Unless you have another lead?"

Lexi didn't.

"It's somewhere to start looking," Boss said. "Trent, can you bring up a map of this place? We need to find the quickest way to the delivery bay."

"On it." Trent unlocked the comms unit on his right forearm and started tapping in commands. A few seconds later he looked up at them and nodded. "We need to take the staff entrance on the west side of this room, then take the service elevator."

Boss grunted. "Let's get going then."

They beat a path between the multiple reception desks and headed towards the far side of the dome. The view overhead was still breathtaking and each of them glanced upwards every couple of steps to take it all in. Lexi thought about the excited families who must have passed through here. Where were they all now? What had happened to them?

At the edge of the dome was a nondescript metal door reading: EMPLOYEES ONLY. There was an electronic keypad beside it.

Boss turned to Trent. "Can you get us through?"

"If Britcomm have provided us with an override, I should be able to get us in anywhere. Let me check the server...okay, yeah, I have it. A dominus sequence that should override everything we encounter."

Boss nodded, satisfied.

Trent linked up to the keypad and overrode it in seconds. The door popped open and they all stepped inside. The following corridor was far more utilitarian than the gigantic dome they were leaving, but it was jazzed up by the odd motivational poster or bright yellow notice. A large cardboard Pip the Explorer stood off to one side with a speech bubble proclaiming: BE A BRIGHT STAR AND SMILE.

Gellar pointed. "The elevator's over there."

"I'll access the controls," Trent said, hurrying ahead.

Hopper looked around and folded his arms. He seemed worried.

"What is it?" Lexi asked him.

"There's nothing left behind. People panic when things go wrong. They drop things, they break things, they shit themselves. This place seems as though everyone just disappeared in an orderly fashion. That makes no sense."

Lexi saw his point. "Something rational must have happened, then. We just need to figure out what it is. Maybe we'll find answers in the delivery bay."

Hopper scratched at his chin. "Maybe."

"Okay, we're in," Trent shouted back at them from the elevator.

They went and gathered inside the large cargo lift and waited for the doors to close. Once they started to descend, a voice came through the speakers. "Arriving at Cargo Bay Level 1. All employees must obey Health and Safety regulations at all times. Enjoy your day."

"I can just imagine what this place is like to work at," Hopper said. "Smile or you're fired. Turn up early for your shift or you're fired. Eat shit or you're fired."

"Nothing wrong with expecting people to do their jobs," Miller said. "People behave like they're owed a living. My father used to build thruster units for space destroyers. He worked twelve-hour days his entire life and I never heard him complain once. Why are people so afraid of hard work?"

"What's the point of being alive," Hopper said, "if it's only to work all day doing something you hate? Your dad spent twelve hours a day building thrusters, why? Because he loved it or because he had no choice? Humanity boxed itself in, working everyone to death so we can all wear the latest watch-tablets on our wrist. It's a stupid way to live, man. Money is the worst thing that ever happened to humanity."

Gellar huffed. "I agree. My mother worked three jobs to clothe and feed my brothers and me. She never got to have any life of her own. I can't help thinking that maybe we should've taken a different path as a species."

Miller rolled his eyes. "Jeez, let's just undo four-thousand years of human history, shall we? People are all given the same opportunities. If they end up miserable then they only have themselves to blame."

"I can't even begin to explain how many shades of bullshit that is," Hopper said.

The elevator jolted.

"We're here," Boss said. "Get your heads in the game."

The doors opened, revealing a brightly lit warehouse that seemed to go on forever. Lexi was beginning to realise that everything at Installation 23 was gigantic. There was no reason to do anything small on the moon.

"This place is incredible," Trent said, looking around in amazement. "They could put enough supplies in this place to restart humanity."

"Maybe that's why this place was really built," Hopper suggested.

Miller snickered. "Yeah, because a theme park on a moon right next to Earth is an ideal place to build a colony. If something ever happened to the Earth, like an asteroid or something, don't you think the moon would be pretty screwed as well?"

Hopper shrugged.

"Any idea where to start looking?" Gellar asked.

Lexi looked around and thought she had an idea. "Over there." She pointed. Up ahead was a group of humanoid units. They were deactivated and slumped over like hump-backed old men.

"Why are they all deactivated?" Hopper asked.

Lexi folded her arms. "Maybe whatever shut off the communication networks shut down the humanoids, too. Don't they run off a relay?"

"Yes," Trent said. "They're all connected and can be shut off together. Something must have knocked out the relay."

"What is that blue crate, there," Gellar pointed to a large, plastic crate that lay at the feet of one of the deactivated humanoids.

"Just a delivery," Miller said. "What's so important about it?"

"The lid is halfway up," Gellar noted, "like the humanoid froze right after it was opened. The man in the video told us to leave. Something bad happened here. Maybe it was something that got delivered."

Boss nodded. "It might be worth checking out."

Lexi swallowed a lump in her throat. "What if it's something dangerous?"

"Then we're probably already screwed," Hopper said. "I'll go check it out."

Boss stopped him. "Gellar is our munitions expert. If it's something volatile, she should be the lead on this."

Gellar didn't looked thrilled at the prospect, but she nodded and started walking. Everyone stayed back while she headed over to the crate. Her steps were jerky, as if she was fighting her own legs and Lexi felt her stomach tighten anxiously as she imagined how tense the American woman probably felt as she walked towards what could be a threat to her life. Lexi had a feeling her father had selected Gellar to perform the task because she was closest to panicking. It was better to have her take an active part in the mission than to have her stand back and let her idle thoughts carry her away.

Gellar stopped in front of the blue plastic crate and covered her mouth. "Oh God!"

Boss stepped forward. "What is it?"

"It's...meat. Disgusting."

The rest of the group quickly joined Gellar and, sure enough, there was what appeared to be a thick slab of festering meat inside the crate, covered with writhing maggots.

Trent gagged. "That's gross."

"It's just a food delivery," Miller said. "It's been left to go bad."

Hopper knelt down beside the crate and made everybody groan by shoving his hand right into the spoiled meat.

Trent covered his mouth. "Dude, that's not cool. Get your hand out of there."

"Just a minute. I see something." Hopper rummaged around, making squelching sounds in the meat and releasing a waft of pungent odour. Eventually, he pulled his arm free again and was holding something in his hand.

Hopper held the object up and looked at Trent. "You know what this is, buddy?"

Trent squinted at the sticky device. "I'm not sure. It looks like a wireless transmitter of some kind. Here, let me take a look." He covered his mouth with one hand while reaching out and taking the unit with the other. "Damn, it's all sticky."

"Be a man," Hopper said. "Not the first time you've had sticky meat in your hands before."

Gellar tutted. "That's disgusting, Hopper."

Hopper winked. "I'll grow on you."

"Like fungus, maybe."

"You're covered in...stuff," Lexi said, pointing at the wet, glistening maggots on Hopper's hands.

"There's a hygiene bay over there," Boss said flatly, pointing off to the corner of the warehouse.

Hopper nodded. "I'll go get cleaned up." He marched away from the group.

Trent was turning the sticky transmitter over in his hands and examining it closely. His revulsion seemed to have passed now that his curiosity had taken over him. "It's a pretty old unit," he said. "A BR13. Commercial use, not military. Main use is remote relay, like sending instructions to an unmanned machine. A drone, mining equipment-"

"Humanoids?" Lexi interrupted.

Trent shrugged. "I guess so. The programmer would need to be pretty skilled to hack one of these units, though. They're state of the art."

Boss folded his arms across his large chest and looked at his daughter. "You think someone sent a signal from this thing to shut down the humanoids, Lexi?"

"Maybe."

Gellar frowned. "For what purpose?"

Lexi shrugged. "To make sure an actual person received the package. The humanoids take deliveries and check them, right? Well, maybe they're programmed to dispose of anything unexpected. Maybe the only way to get this package into the hands of an actual human being was to make the humanoid handlers malfunction."

"I suppose that makes sense," Gellar conceded. "Although it's a stretch."

Miller grunted. "Why work so hard to get a hunk of meat into the hands of a porter? To what end?"

Lexi thought it was obvious, so she explained. "The guy in the video was sick – really sick. I think whatever he contracted, he got from this piece of meat."

Trent looked down at the sticky unit in his hand and suddenly looked very ill. "I think maybe it would be a good idea if we all went and got cleaned up."

Boss nodded. "I think that would be wise.

On their way to the hygiene bay, they were met by Hopper coming the other way. His arms were wet and soapy, but his face was a rigid slab of concern.

"What is it?" Boss asked.

"I found something," Hopper said, both eyebrows raised.

"Found what?"

"A survivor. Sort of."

Everyone got moving.

#

The unknown man was a mess, barely breathing and lying in a hump on top of a crate of blue paper towels. His face was pockmarked with weeping blisters and sores. His lips sucked at the air hungrily but his eyes remained closed.

"Is it the man from the video?" Lexi asked.

Miller shook his head. "No, this is somebody else. He's wearing a janitor's uniform."

"Can you help him?"

Gellar knelt down beside the sick man and placed a hand against his forehead. "He has a fever. From the pustules on his face I would suspect something viral. Antibiotics may work, something to bring down the fever."

"There's a hospital in the guest complex," Trent said. "I saw it on the maps I downloaded onto my comms unit."

Lexi looked down at the sick man. "If there's been some kind of viral outbreak then perhaps the hospital is the smartest place to search."

"Or the stupidest," Hopper said. He was back at the sinks, scrubbing at his skin with watered-down bleach. His skin was red raw, but it was the right idea. If there was something nasty clinging to their skin, then it was worth suffering a chemical burn to get rid of it.

Trent went so far as to wrap a wet rag around his face, making him look like a surgeon. "I think I'd like to get out of here," he said.

"We need to take him with us," Lexi said, motioning towards the sick man. "If he wakes up he could tell us what happened."

"Of course," Boss said. "He comes with us. We're here to help."

"I'm not carrying him," Trent said.

Lexi huffed. "Fine. I will." She got beneath one of the sick man's arms and started to lift him. The act of moving him brought him to consciousness and his eyes fluttered open. He looked around at everyone like he was waking from one nightmare into a new one.

"Don't...don't..."

"Don't what?" Lexi said.

"Don't touch me. Don't touch anyone." With that, the man stiffened, his eyes rolling back in his skull. He seized hard, his body trembling. Then he went still.

Miller felt the man's neck for a pulse, but shook his head. "He's dead. Heart attack, or maybe an embolism. An autopsy would confirm."

"We didn't bring a pathologist with us," Boss said. "So we're going to leave him and get the hell back to the Hermes. We'll report back and request a medical team and a full quarantine operation."

"Sounds good to me," Trent said. "I'm not sticking around to catch whatever this guy had." He lifted the sticky transmitter in his hand and threw it into the sink. "Whatever is going on here is more than we're equipped to handle."

"What did you do that for?" Lexi said irritably. She went over to the sink and retrieved the transmitter. It was soaking wet and covered in bleachy suds.

Trent shrugged. "It's covered in gunk. It might be teeming with the virus."

"It's also part of our investigation. We still don't know what it's for-ouch!" Lexi dropped the sparking unit to the floor where it promptly snapped in two. It spat out a couple more sparks before dying completely.

"Nice one, butterfingers."

Lexi scowled at Trent. "It was already broken because you threw it in the sink."

Then came a noise.

CATASTROPHIC SOFTWARE FAILURE. REBOOTING. CATASTROPHIC SOFTWARE FAILURE. REBOOTING.

Everyone looked around to watch the humanoids. They were straightening up, yellows eyes glowing as they spoke the same message over and over again in unison. CATASTROPHIC FAILURE. REBOOTING.

"They're coming back online," Trent said with a smile on his face. "When the transmitter broke, it must have stopped sending out whatever signal it was jamming them with."

"Will they be able to provide us with information?" Boss asked.

Trent nodded enthusiastically. "Humanoids record and share everything on a virtual network. We only need a single unit online to access everything they've collectively witnessed. If I link up I can give us CCTV, data entries, everything."

"Good," Boss said. "Then we'll have this mystery solved."

Lexi watched the humanoids continue their start-up routines. One of them turned slowly to face her. Its yellow eyes pulsed. Its mouth opened wide like the maw of a snake and a long, drawn-out whistle came from its voice box.

"What's it doing?" Lexi asked, covering her ears and wincing.

Trent shook his head. "I don't know. I...It looks like some kind of data corruption in the start-up Kernel. Let me see if I can access its operating system." Trent switched on his comms unit and headed over to the whistling humanoid. Its eyes continued to pulse like a strobe light.

"I've never seen one do that before," Gellar said.

Lexi looked at her. "Have you been around them much?"

"Yes, the Army used them in my unit for resupply and mine disposal. Before I joined the Space Corp, I was in the field during the Texan-Mexican war. There were dozens of humanoids on the ground with us. They never did this, though."

"I'll figure it out," Trent shouted over the noise. "Just let me plug in." He pulled a zipwire out of his comms unit and plugged it into a small slit-port behind the whistling humanoid's ear. Immediately its eyes stopped pulsing and settled on a solid yellow.

The whistling stopped.

"What did you do?" Lexi asked Trent.

"Nothing yet. I was just about to-"

Trent's feet left the floor as the humanoid grabbed him around the throat and lifted him up. His legs thrashed in the air.

Boss was the first to respond. He dashed forward and grabbed a hold of Trent, tried to pull him free. "Trent, stop screwing around!"

Trent choked and spluttered. "H-help."

The group of humanoids were suddenly all awake. They looked around curiously with their bright yellow eyes like newly-hatched lizards.

"This ain't good," Hopper said.

Lexi ran forward as the humanoids began to converge on her father and Trent. Trent was growing purple in the face and his kicking was becoming more frantic. Boss had started pummelling the humanoid in the face but the blows did nothing. It was like punching a sheet of metal. "I can't get him loose," he shouted as Lexi came to help him.

Lexi grabbed one of the humanoid's arms and tried to yank it away, but it was impossible.

Trent's struggling grew weaker. His eyes bulged from his head.

The other humanoids began to approach en masse.

"We need to get out of here," Miller shouted at them. "Run."

But Lexi kept struggling to free Trent. "We can't leave him."

"You have to," Miller shouted. "Get out of there."

Lexi looked over her shoulder in time to see another humanoid coming right for her. It snatched out a hand and tried to grab her, but she ducked out of the way. Boss was still trying to release Trent, but his hands were bloody from throwing so many punches. Trent had gone still, dangling limply from the vice-like grip around his throat.

Lexi was about to admit defeat. The other humanoids would be on them any second and there was no point her dying trying to save Trent. He was already lost.

"Get down!"

Lexi spun around to see Hopper coming at them with a large yellow bucket. Boss spotted him, too, and got out of the way just in time to avoid the torrent of soapy water being released from the bucket. The water soaked the humanoid and immediately its yellow eyes began to spit sparks.

It released Trent's neck and he crumpled to the floor.

"Help me get him up," Boss shouted.

Lexi and Boss scooped Trent up by his arms and started dragging him away towards the elevator where Miller and Gellar urgently waited for them. Hopper covered their back, kicking out at the humanoids that had begun to give slow, deliberate chase.

Gellar ran forward to meet them all and helped them carry Trent the last few yards, and between the three of them they managed to drag him into the elevator.

Hopper was still outside and they shouted at him to hurry. He was still holding the plastic bucket in his hands and he decided to lob at the nearest humanoid. It bounced off its head uselessly, but Hopper's point was made. He turned around and leapt into the elevator just as the doors were closing.

They started heading upwards. "Arriving at the Space Dome. This is a public area, please ensure all standards of uniform are met. Enjoy your day."

"How did you know that would work?" Lexi asked Hopper between panicked breaths.

Hopper shrugged. "Doesn't matter how far along technology comes, electronics and water just don't mix."

"You knew the eyes were a weak point?"

"They are on a human being. I figured the same might be true for fake humans."

Miller was on the floor, checking on Trent. "He's still alive, but his pulse is weak."

"Is he going to be okay?" Lexi asked.

"Depends on whether or not his neck is damaged. If his windpipe is broken or if the blood was shut off from his brain for too long..." He shrugged. "We'll know as soon as he wakes up. If he wakes up."

The elevator doors opened.

"We need to get Trent somewhere safe," Boss said. "We don't know how many more of those bloody machines are walking around the place."

"They don't use them in the public areas," Lexi said, recalling what she knew of the park. "They break the illusion of fantasy for the guests."

"We should stick to the public areas, then," Gellar said.

"We're heading back to the Hermes," Boss said. "Some sort of cyber-attack has made the humanoids dangerous. That might be what caused everyone to disappear. We're not equipped to deal with a hostile situation like this."

"That's not true," Miller said. "The Hermes is equipped with six battle assault rifles and pulse grenades."

"We're not frikkin' soldiers," Hopper said.

"Gellar and I are Marines."

"Well, you two feel free to go full Rambo, but you won't find me running around with a gun."

"Let's just get to the Hermes," Lexi said. "We'll make a plan from there."

They exited the elevator, carrying Trent between them, and headed back out into the space dome. The view was a lot less awesome this time and, more than ever, Lexi felt the weight of the cosmos bearing down on her. They hurried into the boarding tunnel, where Hopper released the airlock, and they threw themselves back inside the Hermes like the Wrath of God was nipping at their heels.

Hopper closed the airlock and slumped against the wall. "That was hairy," he said.

"Open a comm channel, Lexi," Boss ordered. "I need to get a report to Britcomm ASAP."

Lexi climbed into the cockpit and switched on the Hermes' transmitter. She was surprised when the console failed to light up. In fact the entire cockpit stayed dark. Even the standby LEDs were blank. She swivelled in her chair and tapped at the nav console. That, too, stayed dark.

"What is it?" Boss said, obviously seeing the confusion on her face.

"Nothing's working. The computers, the controls...it's all down."

"How is that possible?"

"It's not," Hopper said, flicking the cabin's light switch on and off uselessly. "Nothing would cause the ship's systems to fail all at once – except for one thing: sabotage. Somebody did this."

"Maybe it's the same thing making the humanoids play up," Gellar suggested.

"Or," Hopper said, "somebody came and uploaded a virus into the computer's base programming or placed an EM jammer nearby to shut down the ship's power core."

The radio unit on Trent's shoulder suddenly hissed and a voice came through it. "You can't leave. You have been exposed.

You must remain here. I'm sorry."

Boss grabbed the radio unit and barked a reply. "Who is this? Identify yourself."

"I'm just a man. A man trying to do what's right. You cannot leave. You're all going to die here. I'm sorry."

The radio went dead, just like everything else around them.

#

"Who the hell was that?" Miller demanded as he opened up a supply cabinet at the rear of the Hermes. From inside, he pulled out an assault rifle and shoved in a magazine.

"Calm down," Boss said, raising his meaty hand.

Miller cocked the weapon and handed it to Gellar, then started loading up a second. "I suggest we arm up. Each magazine holds one-hundred-fifty low-velocity ball bearings. Makes a mess of a man but won't damage anything keeping a roof over our heads."

"I'm with Miller," Gellar said, strapping the assault rifle around her neck. "That was a threat we just received. Our ship has been sabotaged. We need to defend ourselves."

Boss spoke slowly, calmly. "Twenty-thousand innocent people. That's how many lives are in jeopardy here. Running around with rifles isn't going to do very much, but if it makes you two feel better, then by all means take them; but if you fire off a single round without my say so, I will personally see to it that you are Court Marshalled out of your respective units."

Miller scowled. "You have no say in military matters."

Boss walked up to Miller and stood nose to nose with him. "Really? Who do you think taught your General Baxter how to fly? In fact, the very reason I have you and Gellar here is because Baxter owed me a favour. If you want to see how many powerful hands I've shaken, test me."

Miller took a step back and averted his eyes. Gellar looked away too.

"Okay," Boss said, his tone suddenly positive and fatherly. "We're in a spot of bother here, officers, but that's what we've all been trained for. My decision to abort the mission stands. We need to get a call through to Britcomm advising of the situation. That is still our only priority. Our own communications are down, which means we must seek alternatives."

"We should head for the control centre," Hopper said.

Boss nodded. "Yes, we should. I imagine this place has enough technology to light up every cell phone on Earth. We need to head there immediately."

"But the comms are offline," Lexi said. "That's why we're here in the first place."

Hopper folded his arms across his chest. "I bet the guy who threatened us on the radio is behind it. There's someone screwing with all the systems in this place. Maybe it's a tech; someone who works here."

"I don't care who's responsible," Boss said. "I just care about getting to that control room and doing whatever we need to do to get a call out."

"If the systems are down," Lexi said. "Then the only person who can get them working again is Trent."

"Good thing he's awake again," Hopper said, nodding down at their fallen colleague.

Trent blinked, looking at them all in a daze.

"Are you okay, Trent?" Lexi asked. She knelt down beside him and put a hand against his cheek soothingly.

"Did I win?" he said.

Lexi smiled. "Not so much. Do you remember what happened?"

Trent shoved himself up into a sitting position and rubbed his neck. "Yeah, I remember." He looked around at the unlit cockpit, noticed the dark computer displays. "We're in trouble, aren't we?"

"No," Lexi said. "Not yet, but we're going to need your help."

"Okay, but it's somebody else's turn to get strangled by a robot next time."

"Deal. Can you get up?"

Trent said he could, so she helped him to his feet. He swayed dizzily, but managed to stay upright on his own. He eyed the assault rifles that Gellar and Miller held and frowned. "There are two-hundred humanoid units at Facility 23. I hope you've brought enough ammunition."

"We're sticking to the public areas," Lexi said. "They shouldn't be around."

"Let's get going," Boss said. He moved over to the airlock and pulled the release, allowing them all to proceed cautiously back through the tunnel and into the domed check in area. Up ahead, behind all of the desks, was a sloping pathway. At the top the hill was an archway with a huge banner attached to it. It read: WELCOME TO GRAND GALAXY. YOUR ADVENTURE STARTS HERE.

"Get your tickets ready," Hopper told them. "And keep your arms and legs inside the ride at all times."

They stuck close together and started up the slope cautiously. The silence was unsettling. Walking into humanity's largest theme park should not have been a quiet affair. They hopped over the turnstiles and entered into the first section of the amusement park. It was a shopping area, full of themed stores and guest services running in two parallel rows. In the middle of the paved walkway was a pretend spaceship, painted white and red like an ambulance – it was a designated First Aid station. Behind it lay a bank of vending machines set inside a pretend rocket. The ceiling blinked and twinkled with fake stars three hundred-feet above their heads.

"This is all wrong," Trent said nervously. "There should be people everywhere." He rubbed at his neck again. "Although, right now, I'm glad of the peace and quiet."

Boss gave his orders. "Take point, Miller. Gellar, bring up the rear."

They moved in a line, the two soldiers at front and back, and kept their pace slow and cautious. It didn't take long, though, before they encountered the park's first attraction.

Lexi looked up at the looping rollercoaster and couldn't quite believe it. The thing was eighty-feet high and swooped and dove in every direction. The fact that something like this had been built on the moon was hard to conceive, but there it was right in front of here. The coaster's cars were modelled after old-fashioned black and white lunar rockets, like the ones used at the turn of the century. The rollercoaster's journey began with a vertical launch, mimicking a blast-off. The cars shot directly upwards, just like a real rocket launch, before swinging up and over into a series of helices and loops. The ride was designed to look like the guests were leaving Earth and travelling into the cosmos. It looked like a lot of fun."

"Maybe when this is all over we can take it for a spin," Hopper said.

"I'm sure they'll be lifetime passes for all of us," Boss said. "Let's just keep it moving. Trent, you have the maps. Do you know the quickest way to travel to the comms room?"

"It's at the back of the park, near the Forbidden Planet section. Just under a mile ahead."

Hopper whistled. "This place is big."

"You have no idea," Trent said. He was zipping through

information on his comms unit. "Looking at the maps of this place is like looking at a city. It has a water treatment plant, oxygen garden, hospital, supermarket, casino, nuclear power core, trash compaction site...it goes on and on. The amusement park is only a tiny piece of this place."

"What's that?" Lexi pointed at a collection of wooden crates directly in front of them, blocking most of the path.

Trent shook his head. "I don't know."

Before anybody had chance to approach, a ball of flame went hurtling through the air towards them. It struck the wooden crates on the pathway and disappeared inside one of them.

Boss grabbed Lexi and shoved her to the ground. "Get down!" he shouted as he dove on top of her.

There was a massive explosion, followed by assorted sounds of whizzing, popping, and crackling. Lexi looked up from beneath her father to see fireworks erupting from the crates in all directions. The crates themselves were on fire and a candyfloss cart lay on its side nearby, smouldering from the blast.

Boss pushed Lexi's face against the ground, not letting her move. "Sound off!"

"Hopper okay."

"Miller okay."

"Gellar okay."

"Trent...not okay, but I'll live."

Fireworks continued rocketing into the air, exploding above their heads and hitting the store fronts and ride fascia. As Lexi struggled out from under her father and climbed to her feet, a fizzing green ball flew inches past her face.

"What the fuck?" Miller growled, aiming his rifle in all directions. Every firework that popped made him flinch and adjust his position.

"Keep your head together, solider," Boss demanded.

Miller nodded and lowered his rifle slightly.

Another ball of flame flew through the air. Lexi spotted it first and shouted a warning just in time for everyone to take cover.

"Incoming!"

The fiery projectile smashed on the pavement and ignited.

"Somebody's throwing firebombs," Gellar shouted. "Permission to fire."

"Permission bloody well granted," Boss shouted back to her.

Lexi spotted movement. "Over there," she pointed to a man standing inside an asteroid-themed carousel ride twenty yards ahead.

Gellar sought out her target and allowed a smirk to cross her lips. "Target acquired." She pulled the trigger.

Lexi watched as the stranger darted away amidst a hail of deadly ball bearing fire. Miller broke cover and tried to give chase, but the flaming firework crates held him back. "Damn it," he bellowed, firing off a barrage of rounds. "Damn it."

Boss rushed up and slapped the muzzle of Miller's rifle towards the ground. "You have no target. There could be civilians."

"With all due respect, Boss, someone is screwing with us. And I do not like being screwed with."

"Chill the hell out," Hopper said.

Miller turned on him. "Chill out? If it wasn't for me bringing along a rifle we would probably all be toast right by now."

Hopper rolled his eyes. "You're acting like a dick."

Miller went red in the face, but before he responded, Gellar cut him off. "He's right, Miller. Stop flying off the handle. We stick together and we act smart. You're a Marine. Act like one."

Miller seethed, his teeth bared. He turned and walked away.

"What's his deal?" Hopper asked Gellar once Miller was out of earshot.

"A rebel set his brother on fire in the Texan-Mexican war using a Molotov cocktail. I'm assuming he's not a fan of firebombers."

Hopper let his shoulders slump and decided not to say anything else.

Lexi went over to where Miller was standing and stood beside him. Hearing about his brother's fate had upset her. "You okay, Miller?"

"I'm fine. Why is everyone ragging on me for trying to do my job? I'm a soldier. My job is to shoot bad guys."

"I thought a soldier's job was to protect people. You're not protecting us by losing your cool. You were right about bringing the rifle, but that doesn't mean you need to use it every time."

Miller sighed. "Sometimes a rifle is the only tool that works."

"You're a medic. You must have seen that sometimes a rifle does more damage than it needs to."

Miller didn't reply, but he at least seemed to think about it.

Lexi left Miller and went back to the others. The fires were starting to diminish and they were able to edge their way forward carefully and move onto the next section of path. Whoever had attacked them was apparently long gone, but had left in a hurry when Miller and Gellar fired upon him. Stashed up against the side of the carousel was a collection of petrol bombs, along with a Grand Galaxy jacket and another company tablet like the one they'd found at reception desk. Trent grabbed the tablet immediately and used his comms unit to hack into it. A moment later he was smiling.

"What have you found?" Lexi asked.

"CCTV recordings for the park. Looks like the guy was downloading the security feeds. Maybe he wanted to delete them; cover up evidence or something."

"Are they still viewable?"

"Some are."

Boss came over, having heard the conversation. "Good. Let's finally find out what happened to this godforsaken place."

Trent selected the first file within the folder and hit PLAY.

- 3 -

The video feed began at the entry terminal, a hive of activity. People came and people went as normal, no fear or confusion on their faces, only joy and excitement. Trent went ahead and opened several more video files and displayed them all side by side in little windows – the hotel and spa, the amusement park, the casino, the waterpark – but Boss told Trent to keep going until he found a feed from the cargo bay. The only clues they had pointed to the arrival of that mysterious blue crate.

Hopper whistled. "Have you seen how many zones there are? Talk about needle in the frikkin' hay-"

"There," Lexi interrupted. "Trent, you've got it."

Trent brought up the window she was pointing at and everyone leaned in closer to get a look. A small group of warehouse employees milled around the cargo area, moving from bay to bay with clipboards tucked beneath their arms. They were accompanied by fastidiously working humanoids.

Boss pointed towards the top of the screen. "That's where we found the crate full of rotten meat."

Lexi squinted. "Are you sure?"

"Yes. Can we zoom in?"

Trent did as he was asked and zoomed in, but he said, "The

humanoids are still functioning here. I'll fast forward to the point when they go offline"

The humanoids sped up on screen, whizzing around as the video was forwarded, but then suddenly slumped over into the deactivated positions they had been in earlier.

Lexi chewed at her lip.

Hopper said, "Looks like we've found the point where everything screwed up."

One of the humanoids stood by the unopened blue crate and began violently shaking from side to side. A worker appeared, looking very much like the man who had warned them in the first video, and pushed the humanoid aside. He stared at the crate and even scratched his head. It was obvious the man was confused. After looking around for help, he shrugged and turned his attention back to the crate. He ran his fingers over the lid, perhaps reading the label printed on top of it.

"Look at the humanoid," Lexi said.

The humanoid unit had stopped its violent shaking and was now watching the man beside the crate. Its eyes had changed from yellow to red.

Lexi frowned. "What's happening to it?"

Trent shook his head. "I'm not sure."

The man reached into the blue crate, unaware of what the humanoid was doing behind him, and pulled something out of it – a small black device, He seemed disgusted by something that was now coating his arm. He sniffed at his wrist, grimaced, and then peered back inside the crate. Without warning, a chalky, alabaster cloud engulfed the man's face, causing him to drop the small black unit back into the crate, where Hopper would later find it. The man staggered backwards, his hands held to his face, coughing and hacking as he retreated out of view.

"Zoom out," Boss ordered. "Find him again."

Trent did as he was told and managed to find another camera showing the spluttering man. This time there was also another man – one they all recognised as the ill-fated janitor who was now lying dead where they'd found him. He came to his colleague's aid and quickly begun wiping at his face with a rag pulled from his pocket, trying to clean away the chalky substance that had erupted from the crate.

A few seconds later, the janitor dropped the rag and stumbled backwards himself, with his hands to his own face, just like the man who had opened the crate.

"Whoa," Hopper said. "What just happened?"

Lex leaned closer to try and make out what was going on in the grainy picture. "All the billions spent to create this place and they can't afford decent cameras."

"There's some sort of disturbance," Trent muttered. "It must have been the device we found in the crate."

The original man in the video now walked the length of the cargo bay. He was in clear discomfort, coughing with every step. The Janitor rushed over to the sinks, splashing water on his face.

"If that was the man's only interaction with the janitor..." Miller frowned. "Whatever this is highly contagious."

"See if you can pick him back up," Boss told Trent when the man disappeared off camera again. "If he went out into the public sections of the park..."

Trent flicked between the various feeds. Occasionally he'd stumble across the man, but no sooner would they have him, then he would disappear down another corridor or around a sudden corner. Eventually they tracked him down to a room marked: SECURITY.

The man practically fell into the room, his face still buried in his hands. He dropped to his knees and rolled onto his back where he started to writhe about in pain. There was no sound, but it was clear the man was suffering. Then – just like that – he went limp. His hands slumped to his sides.

"Dead?" Gellar mused.

Lexi shook her head. "Can't be. You saw the video log he left. He was sicker than he is now. It was filmed after what we're watching now."

"From now on, this man is Patient Zero," Boss said. "We need to find him – dead or alive."

Trent fast-forwarded the video feed. Ten minutes after the man had dropped to the floor, he suddenly sat bolt upright.

Hopper leaned closer to the screen. "Is he…laughing?"

Patient Zero was definitely laughing. His arms wrapped around his knees and he rocked backwards and forwards, giggling hysterically.

"What the hell has gotten into him?" Gellar asked.

Lexi exhaled. "Nothing good."

Patient Zero got up and went over to the bank of computers in the security room. He lingered in front of them for a moment and then sat down. It seemed like he was recording a video, perhaps the video log they had watched earlier – he certainly seemed much sicker now after only another ten minutes or so. Trent took the opportunity to jog the video forward. Patient Zero zipped all around the room in fast motion – sometimes standing still, other times sitting at the console recording more messages. The creepiest section of the video was when he was standing directly beneath the security camera, staring up at them with a grin on his face. Trent hit fast forward again until Patient Zero disappeared from the room.

"If we go down there," Hopper said. "I'd wager we find his body slumped somewhere. He has to be dead."

"If he isn't, he will be soon," Miller said. "Clearly something was inside that crate that has affected his brain. He's displaying signs of delirium, likely from fever, and his bleeding skin suggests a massive auto-immune response. If not for the incredibly short symptom progression I could name several likely viruses, but this... It's something I've never seen before."

"Great," Hopper said. "Just...great."

-4-

"Where is that security office?" Boss asked Trent.

"It's in the administration sector, past the Forbidden Planet sector."

"Then that's where we're heading. The comms centre is near there as well, right?"

Trent nodded. "It's all bunched together at the back of the facility. There's a monorail that goes there if we head east towards the Ice Lands sector."

"Too risky," Boss said. "We'll stay on foot. I don't trust anything with a computer in this place."

"Okay, then," Miller said, adjusting his rifle strap around his neck. "Let's get moving."

"Eyes open," Boss said. "Gellar, Miller, you see that lunatic who tried to firebomb us, you shoot to kill. If it turns out to be Patient Zero, all the more reason to take him down."

Miller raised his rifle. "Copy that."

They spread out, exploring the park in an advancing line. Lexi headed over to a children's Helter-skelter and glanced up its spiralling staircase. It made a good lookout, so she decided to head on up. First, she shouted out to Gellar to let her know where she was going.

"Okay, be careful," Gellar shouted back.

Lexi started up the clanging steel steps and picked up speed as she climbed. For a moment she felt like a child again, rushing to the top and to leap down the slide screaming. She always dreamed of places like this, as a kid, but her father had always been so busy, hardly ever home. She had never gone to theme parks, let alone somewhere as magnificent as Grand Galaxy.

Halfway up and she was already out of breath. Cosmonauts were fit and healthy, but they had little need for physical endurance. In fact, spending time in Zero-G could make a person weak and frail. She was suffering the consequences now as she huffed and puffed.

A short while later, nearing the top, she started to smell something off. It was a foul odour and made her wrinkle her nose and breathe through her mouth. She had to fight the urge to gag.

The others were still conducting their own searches down below. Gellar was rooting through a topiary garden, passing between bushes shaped like planets and spaceships, and benches built from futuristic tubes. Further on, Hopper and Trent were chatting to one another outside of a dark ride. The octagonal building possessed a banner reading: Intergalactic Agency for Pest Control.

Her father was nowhere to be seen, but there were so many rides and buildings that it would be easy for him to wander out of sight. The same was likely true for Miller, who was also absent from Lexi's view.

Lexi carried on up the last of the steps, covering her nose with her sleeve as the smell got stronger. When she was about to reach the top, she paused and tried to take as deep a breath as she could without gagging, then she stepped up onto the platform.

Part of her had expected to find a body – only a rotting corpse could smell so bad – but what she hadn't been expecting to find was such an abhorrent mess. The female body slumped at the top of the slide was desiccated, torn open in the middle and leaking guts and fluids everywhere.

Reflex took over and Lexi gagged hard, spewing the meagre contents of her stomach onto the metal floor grate. She had come up there for a reason, to survey the area, so she straightened up and went over to the railings, deciding that the body was evidence to be put aside until she had assessed the entire scene. She leaned over and almost threw up again, but managed to calm herself down this time. Breathing slowly, trying not to let the stench overwhelm her, she stared out at the park below.

She managed to spot her father, standing on an elevated queuing platform for a themed Waltzers ride. Lexi could still see Gellar nearby and also spotted Trent and Hopper again; they were still chatting. Miller was again nowhere to be seen.

Lexi stared out further at the next sector of the theme park. The arched entryway named it ASTEROID FALLS and it seemed to be a rocky, water-based area, with a mingling of red canyons and shimmering rivers. The centrepiece was a large flume ride occupied by a dozen boats shaped like life rafts that were intended to travel along the sleepy canyons before being dumped down into the churning waters of a wide rapid.

Lexi finally managed to locate Miller. He was wandering next to a large, spinning contraption called The Driller. He was scanning around with his rifle, desperate to find a target. Stupid fool, Lexi thought. They were all supposed to stick together, but Miller had forged ahead, eager to find his prey. The guy was trigger-happy. Most Space Marines were.

Lexi spotted movement further ahead, almost at the far end of the Asteroid Falls sector. In fact, she spotted a lot of movement. She placed a hand over her eyes and squinted. The park was huge, and what she was seeing could've been happening a half-mile away, but whatever it was it was quickly getting closer.

The park's guests – at least, some of them – about a hundred men and women in total, were stumbling towards Asteroid Falls. Miller would encounter them first, as there was only a rollercoaster and a couple of shops between him and them, but the crowd was moving quickly, like a writhing mass of insects.

Lexi was about to shout out, to at the very least get a warning to Gellar who was right below her in the garden, but before she even got chance to open her mouth, something seized her ankle. She stumbled away from the railing and almost tripped, kicking out to get her ankle free. A scream escaped her lips when she saw the shredded corpse rise up from the ground to face her. There was no way the woman could still be alive. It was impossible.

The woman seized Lexi by the throat and began to squeeze. Lexi squirmed and struggled, even more when the woman tried to bite her face. Blood and guts spilled all over the floor, making it slippery under foot and hard to fight back.

"Lexi?" The shout came from below, from Gellar. There was no way the American would make it up all of the steps in time to rescue her, though.

Lexi was fighting for her life.

She brought her knee up to shove the bleeding woman away, trying to keep the rotten jaws from biting her. Once she had a little breathing room, Lexi used her arms to try and pry the choking hand away from her throat. But the fingers held on like a vice. Lexi was running out of breath, her vision beginning to spot with black patches and twinkling lights. She felt pressure in her forehead as she strained to catch a breath.

The woman made to grab at Lexi with her other arm, but Lexi ducked. She was still unable to get free of the hand around her throat, though, and began to tremble as she started to lose consciousness. Her knees buckled and she stumbled backwards, dragging her attacker with her. The woman tried to bite her again, this time lunging at Lexi with her entire bodyweight. Lexi's legs completely gave way and she fell to the ground. Her momentum dragged her attacker off balance with her and the woman tumbled forwards. She hit the safety rail and carried right on over the top of it. Her arm twisted and snapped off at the elbow, the hand remaining around Lexi's throat, but the rest of her went plummeting out of sight.

Lexi took a desperate gasp of air. The hand around her throat had gone limp, the fingers no longer squeezing. She tore the disgusting thing away from her and tossed it aside.

Gellar appeared at the top of the steps finally, panting hard and looking panicked. She had her rifle at the ready. "Are you okay?"

Lexi rubbed her throat and took deep breaths. "No, I'm not okay. A dead woman just attacked me."

Gellar raised an eyebrow. "What did you just say?"

"There's no time to explain." Lexi hopped up and went over to the railing. The horde of men and women were still getting closer, almost on top of Miller now. The soldier was still searching around, oblivious to the approaching crowd.

"Who are those people?" Gellar asked, joining her at the railing.

"I don't know, but Miller is about to find out. We need to warn him."

-5-

Lexi got down the spiral staircase twice as fast as she had gone up it. Gellar was right behind her, shouting into her radio. "Miller, come in, over... Damn it, he's not answering."

"Keep trying," Lexi urged, heading away from the Helter-skelter and towards where she had last seen Trent and Hopper chatting. She was glad to find them still there.

Hopper saw her racing towards him. "Whoa, what's wrong?"

"There's a crowd of people coming right our way. Miller is in the next sector. They'll be on him any minute."

Trent frowned. "A crowd? Do you mean the park guests?"

"I don't know. A woman attacked me at the top of the Helter-skelter. If the people coming towards Miller are the same as she was..."

"Okay," Hopper said. "Let's go get him."

"Where's my dad?" Lexi asked, then corrected herself. "Where's Boss?"

"I'm here," he said, marching up behind them. "I heard what you said. Are you okay?"

Lexi noticed the blood stains on her suit and nodded. "It's not mine. We need to go."

"Then let's go."

"I'll keep trying him on the radio," Gellar said as they all chased after Lexi. They reached the edge of the sector they were in and passed through the tall archway leading to Asteroid Falls.

Lexi shouted out. "Miller! Miller, where are you?"

Gellar took point, passing her radio to Trent, and leading with her rifle. She scanned left and right as the group passed by the side of a 4D simulator shaped like a broken-down all-terrain bus. Mad Manny's Thunder Tour.

The path widened up ahead but was bordered on either side by fake canyon walls. Overhead, a false ceiling gave the illusion of being beneath three blazing suns. The claustrophobic walkway stretched for almost a hundred metres and there were food vendors and gift shops nestled inside rock like caves on either side.

Lexi shouted again. "Miller!"

Miller appeared at the opposite end of the canyon, looking back at them. He was so far off that he appeared small.

Trent tried him on the radio but got no answer. "Why isn't he answering? Does he even have his radio on him?"

"He's turned it off," Gellar said confidently. "He's hunting and doesn't want his radio squawking and giving away his position."

Boss growled. "The fool."

"He's the one being hunted," Lexi said. "He just doesn't know it yet."

Miller started heading towards them. It was impossible to make out his expression from so far away, but from the way he moved he looked angry. Perhaps he didn't like having his name shouted.

There was a flash of movement at the very beginning of the canyon, about a dozen metres behind Miller. He had his back to the movement, but Lexi saw it clearly. Someone had flitted past the far entrance to the canyon, moving in and out of view rapidly.

"Miller, run!" she shouted.

But it was too late.

Bodies funnelled into the canyon behind Miller, bunched so close together that they almost moved like liquid; men and women scurrying over one another as they advanced rapidly down the enclosed canyon. Their clothes were torn rags. Many of them were half-naked. They were not friendly. They were like the woman who had attacked Lexi on top of the Helter-skelter. Dead people.

Miller finally heard the stampede behind him and spun around. He threw himself backwards on his heels in shock and quickly brought up his rifle and fired. The sound of the rifle clacking echoed of the canyon walls like thunder and the stream of ball bearings shredded through the bodies like a water jet through leaves, tearing off limbs and disintegrating bone.

But the horde kept on coming.

The torn, bleeding bodies were unstoppable, surging forward like a single organism until they enveloped Miller. His rifle pointed into the sky and continued firing but within a second he was gone, replaced by swarming bodies.

"Get your arses moving," Boss yelled.

Nobody needed asking twice. They turned tail and ran for their lives. The sound of chaos bore down on them, a thousand rabid footsteps echoing off the canyon walls. They were halfway inside the narrow chasm. Trapped. They could head only in one direction, towards the entrance they came from, which meant they were in a life or death sprint with a horde of monsters at their backs.

Lexi was no runner and started falling behind. Gellar looked back and noticed her flagging; then did a crazy thing and stopped. She raised her rifle and started taking shots.

"Gellar, move," Lexi shouted at her.

"You keep on. I'll buy us a few yards." She carried on firing, even as Lexi raced right by her.

Lexi doubled down and caught up with the others. Her father glanced sideways, reached out and grabbed her shoulder. "Come on," he said, "you can't help her now."

They shot out of the canyon like bullets from a gun and lost their bearings as they suddenly found themselves back in the open. They stumbled around, looking for a place to go.

Hopper threw out an arm. "This way."

They ran towards the giant log flume. It was built on top of a fake mountain range and Hopper was the first to grab a handhold and start pulling himself up. "Start climbing," he shouted down to them.

The horde spilled out of the canyon like pus from a wound, squirting in all directions. Lexi leapt at the fake mountain and started clawing her way upwards. Her fingers ached within seconds but she ignored the pain and kept pulling herself upwards. At one point she dared looked down and saw that the horde of dead men and women were swarming beneath her feet like ravenous piranhas. But they didn't climb after her. They leapt and snatched, but seemed unable to grasp the rock with any sort of timing.

The top of the fake mountain was a good fifty feet in the air, and Lexi was the last to reach it. By the time she dragged herself up onto the ledge, Trent, Hopper, and Boss were already waiting for her and helped pull her up. Sweat poured from them all.

"That was frikkin' crazy," Hopper said.

Lexi slumped down onto her knees and tried to catch her breath. Boss knelt down beside her and patted her back. "We're safe," he assured her. "They didn't climb up after us."

"G-Gellar." she said.

Boss exhaled. "If she isn't here now, I don't think she's coming."

"She stayed behind to buy us time."

Hopped growled. "Damn Americans, always so brave. It makes me sick. Miller stood his ground, too, when he should have run like a screaming child."

Trent stared down at the rocks beneath his feet. "Damn, Gellar's really dead. I think she had the hots for me."

"I...do...not!"

Everyone looked around to see a hand gripping the top of the rocks. Hopper rushed over to help Gellar up onto the platform and seemed ecstatic to see her alive. She was bleeding from a wound on her neck, but seemed like she would be okay. She was out of breath, but quickly marched up to Trent and pointed her finger in his face. "Believe me, you're not my type. Tell you the truth, the only one who even comes close is Lexi."

Trent frowned, then opened his mouth. "Oh...."

Lexi blushed, but overcame it by going over and giving the woman a hug. "You brave fool. Thank you."

"Hey, until we get off this godforsaken tourist trap, we're all teammates. I lost my rifle. Those people are savages. They swarmed Miller like... I don't know what. And one of them bit me right on the neck."

"I don't think they're people anymore," Lexi said. "One tried to bite me, too, on the helter-skelter. The woman's stomach was all torn out, and I think she was...dead."

Hopper put his hands to his face. "Great! Frikkin' space zombies. Are you kidding me?"

"What are you talking about?" Boss said impatiently.

Hopper removed his hands from his face. "Er...space zombies? Dead people walking around in space. What would you call them?"

Boss suddenly seemed unsure of himself. "I don't know, but certainly not space zombies."

"Let's just call them dead people, for now," Lexi said.

Hopper nodded. "Fair enough. So we know what happened to the guests now, but we don't know why. How do we avoid being eaten and get our arses home?"

"The plan still stands," Boss said. "We get to the comms centre. We radio Earth and get a team here. If we can manage to remove whatever jam has been targeted at our ship, we may be able to evacuate."

Trent was shaking his head and looked anxious. "So, after getting ourselves all the way to the comms centre, we then get to turn right back around and head all the way back?"

Hopper ran a hand through his hair. "Hoping all the way that the crazy guy in the video doesn't just reactivate the jam while we're on our way back to the Hermes."

"We need to kill him," Gellar said. "If we have any chance of getting out of here in the Hermes, we need to take out the madman who sabotaged it."

There was a brief silence, before Boss admitted, "You're right, but we have no weapons and no clue where he is. We'll just have to hope for the best while preparing for the worst."

"How do we get down from here?" Lexi asked. The platform they were on was a lonely plateau beside the ride's log flume. About fifty-feet ahead, the river suddenly dropped over a crest and plunged towards the ground where the…dead people…would be waiting.

"We're safe up high," Trent said. "We should stay up here."

"We can't live on top of a fake mountain forever," Hopper said. "We're not gnomes."

"Help will come," he said, although in no way confidently.

Boss grunted. "Perhaps, but how long are we willing to wait? There may be survivors here that need our help. We have a duty."

"I'm just a technician," Trent blabbered. "It's not my job to rescue people."

Lexi shook her head at the coward. He'd been little different back at the academy. She remembered once how he had refused to jump from the high dive above the swimming pool during the first stages of their pilot training. It had taken him a month longer than everybody else to finally take the plunge, and he had almost failed. "No, you're right," she said. "It's not your job to rescue people. It should just be a part of you being a human being. You're talking about waiting for people to come and rescue us, but what about the people waiting for us to rescue them?"

Trent said nothing. He just looked over the edge of the fake mountain, with a face that looked like it was going to vomit.

"Guess we take the river then?" Hopper said and, without saying another word, he stepped over the edge and plunged into the calmly moving water. He dove forwards and went beneath the surface, rising a second later, shuddering. The water only went as high as the bottom of his chest. "Least it ain't deep," he said.

Boss looked down at Hopper and sighed. "Do you ever think things through?"

"I prefer to get things done. Come on, there's no other way, so get it over with. The water's fine."

Lexi shrugged and hopped over the edge, landing in the water beside Hopper. The others followed quickly and, before long, they were all wading along the river. The Forbidden zone lay beyond Asteroid Falls and that was where they were headed. They needed to get there quickly, before anything else tried to kill them.

-6-

They came to a stop when they reached the log flume's lift-hill. The water stopped to give way to a pair of winch chains that ran along a steel track. At the bottom was the ride's queue hut. The small shack looked empty and Lexi prayed that it was. The horde from the canyon had lost sight of them atop the fake mountain and it seemed like they might have managed to sneak away.

Lexi and the others dragged themselves out of the water and onto the metal catwalk that ran down alongside the lift-hill. Lexi had to help Gellar, since the American had begun to favour her left side since becoming wounded.

"You okay?" Lexi asked her.

"Yeah, just haven't got a lot left in the tank." She admitted it with a smile.

"Everyone, keep a low profile," Boss said.

They each stooped down and began creeping down the hill towards the shack. They flinched when they entered the small building, but gave a collective sigh of relief when they realised that the massive monster coming through the wall wasn't real, just a prop. The giant sandworm, with rows upon rows of teeth, was just part of the ride theming. It had a horn on its head the size of a golf club.

"Looks like my grandmother," Hopper said as they passed by it.

Lexi wondered how Hopper could stay so upbeat and keep cracking jokes. Either he wasn't afraid or he didn't understand the seriousness of the situation. A third option was that he didn't care about dying.

Boss headed over to the exit and poked his head around the edge of the doorway, but pulled back immediately. "There's one of them out there," he whispered

"Just one?" Lexi whispered back.

Boss nodded. "Looks like."

"They don't make any sound," Gellar said. "If we take it out, we should be able to move on by."

Lexi frowned. "If we take it out? Should we really refer to them as it?"

Gellar shrugged. "Call 'em what you like. All I see is an obstacle that needs dealing with."

"I'll do it," Hopper said. He pulled a short dagger from a sheath on his belt.

Lexi was surprised. "You carry a knife?"

"A pilot never knows when he's going to encounter space pirates. Knife comes in handy."

Gellar huffed. "You think a knife is going to keep you safe from pirates?"

"It ain't for them."

Boss sighed. "I don't see another way, so if you want to volunteer then so be it. Just come back in one piece."

Hopper nodded and headed out the shack. He held the knife out in front of him and looked like he knew how to use it. Lexi wondered if the blade had ever seen use before. The rest of them huddled in the doorway. Lexi was ready to rush out and help the second things went bad, but she silently prayed that they wouldn't.

Hopper's target was a middle-aged man in bloodstained shorts and a Fast and Furious 27 t-shirt. He also wore a torn, plastic poncho with the words Kopper Kanyon Escape printed on it.

Hopper stayed low, kept himself behind the dead tourist, and managed to get right up behind without being spotted. He rose slowly, bringing up his knife...

...

He seized the man around the neck from behind and plunged the knife into his heart. Then he pulled it free and stabbed again. And Again.

But the dead man did not die. He thrashed and kicked, tried to bite at Hopper's forearm that was wrapped around his throat. Hopper kept stabbing, making a mess out of the man's torso, but the wounds were having no effect. The dead man kept on fighting.

Lexi saw the panic in Hopper's eyes as he struggled to hold on. Beside her, Trent was hissing. "That stupid idiot. The only way to kill a zombie is by attacking the head."

Lexi turned to him. "What?"

"The head! You have to attack the head and destroy the brain. Nothing walks around without a brain, not even a dead man."

Lexi looked around for a solution and thought she spotted one back where they'd come from. She ran over and seized the horn on top of the giant sandworm's head and pulled with all her strength. The thing was made of steel, but the sandworm's head was fibreglass. It creaked and moaned as she worked to get the horn free and, when she began bashing at it with her fist, it eventually began to lean.

The steel rod broke free.

Lexi sprinted back to the exit, where she now found her father trying in vain to help Hopper. The two of them each held one of the struggling dead man's arms. If he made a noise, he could attract more of his kin, but fortunately he remained silent, even as he thrashed and battled to get free.

Lexi held the steel rod out in front of her like she was going to use it for pole-vaulting, but as she closed in on the dead tourist, she raised it over her shoulder and thrust it towards his face. The spike slid in through the eye-socket and went all the way out the back of the skull. The dead man stopped moving.

Hopper and Boss hopped back as the body slumped to the floor at their feet. When it hit the ground, the dead man's skull exploded and released a tide of black mush.

"Damn. Something liquefied his head," Trent said with a grimace.

"Good work, Lexi," Boss said. "We were beginning to lose the battle there."

"It was because of Trent. He said we have to attack these things in the head. He knew what to do."

Trent straightened up and looked proud.

"Makes sense," Gellar said. "When I stopped to fire on them, they just kept on coming. Eventually, I had to throw down my rifle and get out of there." She pressed a hand against her wounded neck. "I only just managed to."

"We need to get moving," Boss said. "The Forbidden Zone is up ahead. I saw it from up on the mountain. We need to get to that comms room."

"What if there're more of those things?" Trent said.

"Then we stay out of their way. Or we run."

Gellar pointed. "I think the way is clear over there."

There was a path leading off to the left. It passed through an eating area and seemed quiet, deserted.

"Let's move quickly," Boss said.

When they reached the small courtyard between the various restaurants, Hopper dragged himself over to a burger hut, skipping over the counter and rummaging around the back. The scrolling menu screen listed the extortionate prices as if it were still business as usual. It gave a strange sense of normality against everything they had seen.

"What are you doing?" Lexi asked.

Hopper grabbed a paper cup from a dispenser at the back, then brought it to the front where there was a row of taps. He pulled one of the handles and released a flow of draught cola. He filled the cup up to the brim and then downed the contents. Gasping, he said, "I've been so busy trying not to die that I forgot how thirsty I was. Can I get anybody anything?"

Despite the lingering danger, everybody rushed over to the counter and placed an order. Hopper poured them all their beverages of choice and then topped them up again once they were empty. It made a difference. Everybody seemed a little less near breaking point now.

Lexi smiled at Hopper. "You'd make a good barman."

"I'd make a good anything," he said.

Lexi chuckled. Somehow Hopper's arrogance wasn't offensive, perhaps because it might well be true.

"Hello again, my friends."

Everybody stood back as the burger hut's menu screen was taken over by the face of a man they all recognised.

-7-

"Trying to leave this place or contact Earth is no longer possible," said the man on the screen. Like before, he seemed extremely unwell. His eyes wept a bloody substance and the sore on his cheek had spread down to his lips and chin. Despite the grimness of his condition, however, he spoke with confidence and clarity.

"My name is John Cog and I am a warehouse employee for Grand Galaxy Amusement Park. While my pay grade is low, I have found myself with the unfortunate task of having to take authority over this installation. No one can leave."

Lexi shook her head and shouted at the screen in frustration. "Why? What has happened here?"

Cog blinked his swollen eyelids slowly and sighed. It was unclear whether or not he could hear anything until he gave a reply. "Do you really need to know what happened here to understand what must happen? No one here must be allowed to travel back to Earth. No one from Earth must be allowed to come here. Death is all around you and it will cling to you all. This facility has been attacked. By whom, I do not know, but it was I who opened Pandora's box. I let this thing out, and I cannot allow it to hurt any more people than it already has." Cog started coughing then and spattered the camera lens with black mush.

"Who did this?" Boss demanded. "We need to retaliate."

Cog caught his breathe and shook his head sadly. "The package was sent anonymously and a dozen nations could be responsible. I have learned things in the past few days. Things that make the true nature of this place clear to me. If the rest of the world knew what Britain and America were really doing here…" he started coughing again. He cleared his throat and stared into the camera. "Who did this is not important. What matters is that it all ends here. If you do not see that now, you will soon. They are coming for you now."

The screen went black for a few seconds then reverted back to displaying the food shack's menu.

Lexi closed her eyes and thought. "What did he mean? What is the true nature of this place?"

Boss cleared his throat, looked away. "He's insane. Whatever sickness has found its way into him has warped his mind."

"He seemed pretty sane to me," Hopper said. "It's not like he's making shit up. There are dead people walking around, and we all saw what happened when he opened that crate in the cargo bay. This was an attack."

Gellar sighed. "What better place for a terrorist to attack than the happiest place in the galaxy?"

Trent was chewing at his nails. He pulled them away long enough to say, "He said they were coming. Who is coming?"

As if to answer his question, there was a ruckus nearby as one of the park's bins rolled over onto its side. Standing behind it was a dead man, who was quickly joined by a dozen others.

Hopper leapt back over the counter to join the others. "Oh, for fuck's sake. Not this again."

The dead charged forwards like an army. Lexi started running, eager to get a head start, and the others quickly followed. They passed into the Forbidden Zone, which was designed to look like a Martian wasteland. There was real sand piled underfoot, which made keeping up speed a chore. Fortunately, it also made their undead pursuers less surefooted and many of them tumbled as their ankles twisted beneath them.

"We need to find shelter," Boss said.

"There's a building over there," Trent pointed.

They headed towards a giant citadel, an alien castle seeming to rise from the very sand itself. The entrance was a wide arch, but as they got closer, Lexi could see a metal gate folded up on one side. They might be able to lock themselves inside. She glanced back and saw that the dead were still giving chase, enough of them managing to make it across the sand to completely tear the group of cosmonauts apart.

Hopper made it into the citadel first and quickly turned to face the others. They shot past him one by one until they were all inside.

"Get that bloody gate closed," Boss shouted.

Lexi went back to help Hopper who had made a dash for the metal gate. It didn't take long to realise they were screwed.

Hopper howled. "It's locked."

The padlock was thick.

The dead were right outside.

"Stand back!"

Lexi spun around to see a man running at her with an axe. She was taken so much by surprise that all she could do was stand there and scream. But the man ran right past her and swung the axe at the padlock. It popped free and clattered to the ground.

The first dead man made it inside the citadel and lunged at Hopper, going for his throat. The mysterious stranger swung his axe again and lopped off the dead man's head with a single blow.

"Get gate shut," he said in an East European accent.

Hopper grabbed a hold of the gate and Lexi helped him. It was thick and heavy, but once they got it out of its gutter it began unravelling easily.

A dead teenager with massive hoop earrings came at Lexi, forcing her to let go of the fence and defend herself. She ducked out of the way and kicked the girl in her knees. She went to the ground awkwardly but was quickly climbing back up to her feet again. Lexi moved back to the gate and continued trying to get it shut.

While the stranger with the axe took out another couple of the dead attackers, two dozen more where heading in from the distance. Hopper and Lexi managed to get the gate closed to within a few inches, but left it open a few inches and called out to their mystery saviour.

"Come on," Lexi shouted. "Get inside."

The man swung his axe into a fat Chinese man and then turned and ran. He slipped himself through the gap they had left for him and then Hopper shoved the gate all the way closed and pulled down a locking lever. He gave the gate a tug then stepped away, satisfied. "I think it will hold."

Lexi flinched as a dead man threw himself against the gate. "I hope so."

"Come on," the stranger told them. "If we get out of sight, they should move on. They not sharpest bunch."

"Who are you," Boss asked as they regrouped and headed deeper into the sand citadel. The inside was laid out like the catacombs of an burrowing insect. There were a couple of restaurants and shops near the entrance, but further on was a large queuing area for a ride called The Tunnels of Braxis. Braxis, it would appear from the posters on the walls, was some sort of beastly creature that dwelled within the dark pits beneath the sands. Lexi got a chill thinking about what the thing would look like close up.

"My name is Norman," the stranger told them. "I come here on company vacation. I the only one left."

"You mean the only one left from your company?" Lexi asked.

"No, I mean only one left. Everyone dead, yes? Or they kind of are. They've taken to walking around, yes?"

"Yeah, we noticed," Hopper said. "Do you know what happened?"

Norman shrugged. "I know what happen in the sense that I see everything descend into madness, but I no actually know what happen, if you catch my drift, yes?"

"We think it started inside the cargo bay," Lexi said. "There was an unmarked package and when someone opened it, all the humanoid units shut down and people started getting sick."

"Make sense," Norman said. "Humanoid programmed to protect humans – I know because my company use them for shipping and packing – but they haven't done anything since everything started. Last one I see was doubled over like it had tummy ache."

"They're back online now," Trent said, "But they've been corrupted."

Hopper huffed. "Technology, aye? Gotta love it."

"So tell us what happened, Norman," Lexi urged.

"Okay, but first we move somewhere safe. Gate might not hold forever if they decided to make lingering. Your friend look like she need sit down." He was pointing to Gellar.

Gellar waved a hand. "I'm fine. One of those things took a bite out of me."

Norman looked at her suspiciously but didn't say anything.

"Where should we head?" Boss asked.

"Down here." He pointed to the entrance of the Tunnels of Braxis. "It is closed and secure and fire exit at back will take us away from nasties outside. You people have somewhere you want go?"

"The comms room," Boss said.

Norman nodded. "Okay. No idea where that is."

"It's at the rear of this zone," Trent said, "accessed through a staff area inside a Mexican restaurant."

Norman's face lit up. "I know place. Fire exit take us out right by it. Are you going call for help?"

Boss patted the man on the back. "Damn right we are."

"Good. Because I was go say, if you people rescue party, you are sucking a lot."

Nobody said anything.

Norman opened up the entrance to the tunnel ride and allowed them all to pass through into the dark chamber ahead. The sound of dripping water and whistling wind was being piped in from somewhere and in various places the sandy rock seemed to grow. A spotlight shone in one area where the shadow of a scorpion skittered back and forth.

Hopper giggled. "This place is trippy. Look over there. Can you see that pile of bones sticking out of the dirt?"

"This is reception part of ride," Norman explained. "I was standing in here with my co-workers when first person attack. People very ill that day – you see it all around; folks sneezing and coughing. It was late afternoon when bunch of people cramped inside this passage start screaming. One of the ride actors – guy dressed like an old fashioned archaeologist with whip and hat – grab this little kid and start chowing down on his face. The father try to intervene but some lady take him down. Pretty soon whole room filled with blood and I ran and hide. Eventually things go quiet, and when I sneak out, everyone was gone. The people, the bodies...all gone. I find myself this axe beside fire escape and hid out in restaurant where you find me. That all I know. A lot of big help, huh?"

"It's good just to have you alive," Boss said. "If we get just a single person out of this place in one piece then our mission has been worth it."

"That still seems easier said than done right now," Hopper muttered.

"So why not entire army here?" Norman asked. "Why only send you?"

"Because Earth doesn't know," Boss told him. "Someone got into the comms room and shut off all communications. All we knew back on Earth was that something had happened. No one had any idea..."

Norman sighed. "Yeah, how could anyone imagine this place go all space zombie?"

Hopper chuckled.

"We don't use the term 'space zombie'," Lexi said gently when she saw her father's disapproving frown."

"Fair enough." Norman led them through to a wider area that had been set out like an old tomb. There were three large sarcophaguses in the centre of the room and they each held four seats inside.

"Are we supposed to get in?" Lexi asked.

Norman chuckled. "Maybe, if you want full experience. Might be better if we walk, though, yes? Come on, through here."

Norman walked over to the wall and pushed. It turned out to be a plastic curtain painted to blend in with the walls. Behind it was a track, which the sarcophaguses were obviously meant to run on. Lexi shifted as a draft escaped the tunnel ahead, but when she thought about what was behind her, she had no problems forging ahead.

-8-

Water streamed down the cavern walls on both sides and hot air blew in from overhead. Lexi wiped a sheen of moisture from her forehead and didn't know if she was just hot or if claustrophobia was setting in.

"It open up and is little cooler up ahead," Norman assured them.

Boss spoke. "So, Norman, how long ago did the events you described take place? Communications were lost less than twenty-four hours ago."

"It happen a little before that, I think. Attacks I see, happened yesterday, yes, a little earlier than it is now. I not sure why nobody able to send out SOS. You say something jam all radios?"

"Yes. We found a device inside the cargo bay that seemed to be jamming the humanoids, but the communications blackout was likely instigated from the comms room itself."

Norman sniffed. "Strange. Instead of radioing for help, someone stop all communication. Who would do this thing?"

"That's what we want to find out," Lexis said.

Huffing and puffing caused her to turn around. Gellar was limping along and clutching her neck. She'd didn't look good.

"Gellar, do you need us to stop?"

"No...no. I'm fine. I just..."

Boss saw the condition she was in and put up his hand. "Okay, let's take five."

Lexi helped Gellar over to an outcropping of rocks and sat her down. The wound on her neck glistened and leaked brown, sticky fluid.

"We need to complete our mission," Gellar said firmly.

Hopper came on over and said, "They'll be time for that, Gellar. We need to look after each other first. You look like shit."

Gellar sneered. "Thanks."

"You're welcome."

"What happen to her?" Norman asked.

Lexi turned around to answer him. "She took a stand when we were all under attack. She bought us all time but one of the dead people bit her."

"She's a frikkin' hero," Hopper added, not sarcastically, but very much disapprovingly. Lexi thought it strange, as he was a bona fide, selfless hero himself.

"I'm a soldier," Gellar said, trying to stand up – but being forced back down by Lexi. "I have a mission."

Hopper shook his head. "What mission, Gellar? Our mission is to get off this rock in one piece. You're not going to get very far if you pass out on us."

Gellar shook her head, equal parts confused and irritated. The clamminess of her cheeks and redness to her eyes made Lexi wonder if the American was beginning to hallucinate. "No," she said, but didn't say anything else.

Boss was staring at Gellar intently, his brow furrowed into strips. Lexi went over to him, placed a hand on his arm and snapped him out of his daze. "You okay?"

"What?"

"I said, are you okay?"

"Yes, Lieutenant, I'm fine."

"Maybe we should take a diversion and find the hospital," she suggested, trying to hide her upset at him regarding her by rank and not the fact she was his daughter.

Boss shook his head. "It's too much of a risk. If we run into more of the infected guests we could all end up dead. No, we need to proceed to the comms centre and request rescue."

Lexi understood her father's reasoning, but it was unlike him. Usually his first priority would be to help an injured squad member, not continuing on with the mission.

"Okay," Lexi said. "Maybe we can find a First Aid station en route."

Boss didn't answer. He had gone back to staring at Gellar.

Gellar herself seemed a little better now that she'd taken a breather. She stood up and brushed herself off. "Time to get going again," she said firmly.

"You sure?" Hopper asked.

"Yes. We're wasting time sitting here."

Boss nodded. "I agree. Let's continue the mission."

Lexi frowned, but ended up shrugging her shoulders.

"This way," Norman said, pointing forward.

They followed the tracks through the cavern until they entered into a wider area. Like Norman had said, it was cooler now. The larger cavern was littered with bones. They lay in great, huge piles, some climbing all the way up to the ceiling like grizzly totems. Lexi walked backwards whilst tuning in a circle, taking it all in. Animatronic bats chirped overhead and some even swooped along invisible zip-wires.

"Look out! Don't step there."

Lexi flinched at Norman shouting at her, but was too late to stop her ankle striking something and sending her tumbling down onto her butt.

There was an almighty roar.

Lexi screamed as a spider the size of an elephant descended upon her. Its red glaring eyes bore into her while its spindly legs thrashed wildly. Arms grabbed her from behind and dragged her backwards just as the giant beast landed on the ground where it would have crushed her flat. The spider reared up on its back legs and hissed at her, then leapt away and disappeared behind the rocks.

"What the hell?" she yelled. "What the goddamn hell?"

"It's okay," Hopper said, clutching her tightly and making her look at him. There was a look of amusement on his face, but he did not allow himself to laugh. "It's just part of the ride."

"You hit track switch with foot," Norman told her, a slight chuckle to his words. "You just have close encounter with Braxis.

Lexi looked around for the giant spider but it was gone, obviously resetting itself back into position for the next batch of riders – or whoever was clumsy enough to stumble into the trigger.

"That was the scariest thing I've ever seen in my life," she said. "I nearly wet my pants."

Hopper helped her to her feet. "It was the coolest thing I've ever seen."

Norman was quick to apologise when he saw she was not calming down. "I should have thought to warn you. When ride cars pass by they hit switch that activate Braxis. He leap down and give riders scare of their life, yes?"

"I'm not a rider," Lexi said, her nerves still fraught. "I'm a pedestrian."

Hopped punched her on the arm. "No harm done. People usually pay a fortune to meet Braxis, so consider yourself lucky."

"If you all follow me," Norman said. "I try to let you know if anything else is poised to jump out at you."

They exited Braxis's feeding chamber and went into another tunnel. That tunnel eventually led to a vast pond, lit by torches all around. There were a bunch of dead archaeologists scattered all around and a slithering beast would break the surface of the water periodically and snap its wide jaws. The ride tracks disappeared beneath the water, too – apparently at this part of the ride the sarcophaguses turned into boats.

"Fire exit this way," Norman said.

They followed him to a door hidden behind a shredded canvas tent. They had to step over a life-like mannequin corpse to get to it.

"Does this lead directly outside?" Boss asked.

Norman nodded.

"Then we need to be prepared."

Norman had his axe, but nobody else had anything to defend themselves with. Gellar stooped down gingerly and picked up a fire extinguisher from its pod beside the door. She struggled to hold it up and the pain was clear on her face.

"Here, give it to me," Lexi said.

Gellar seemed embarrassed at being so incapacitated, but she handed over the extinguisher without argument. It wasn't even that heavy, Lexi discovered. Gellar must be hurting badly.

"If we find somewhere with medical supplies, we'll get you patched up, Gellar."

Gellar nodded weakly.

"Everybody ready?" Boss was standing by the door.

Everybody was.

Boss shoved it open and looked outside. "It's clear."

They all funnelled out quickly. The coast was indeed clear.

The Forbidden Oasis stood twenty metres away. It was a pavilion full of posh restaurants and bars, including the one they had been searching for – Outpost Mexicana.

Trent pointed. "The entrance to the comms building is through the back of there."

"But you're never going to make it," said a voice.

Followed by a gunshot.

-9-

Trent tilted and fell backwards like a board. The hole in his forehead was only the size of a pencil, but the back of his head leaked blood all over the floor.

More gunshots and this time it was Boss who reeled back. He spun around, holding his shoulder, and then dove down behind a picnic bench. Hopper had disappeared from sight the moment the first shot rang out, but Gellar and Norman both still stood out in the open.

Lexi dropped the fire extinguisher in her arms, ran towards Gellar, and shouted at Norman. "Get in cover!"

Norman dropped his axe and flung himself facedown onto the ground, but was still out in the open. The fool had not found anything to hide behind. There was no time to help him, so Lexi grabbed a hold of Gellar and dragged her back inside the fire exit they had just stepped out of.

"Did you see who's shooting at us?" she asked Gellar.

Gellar's eyes rolled about in her head and she moaned.

"Gellar, are you still with me?"

She moaned again.

"Damn it." Lexi was on her own. She peered out of the doorway and tried to get eyes on the shooter. She spotted him immediately and recognised him almost as quickly. It was the man from the videos, Cog. His entire face was crisscrossed with bulging black veins, but he held the pistol in his hands steadily as he let off another shot. The bullet struck the picnic table her father was hiding behind. Boss had already taken a bullet. Was he okay? Trent certainly wasn't – dead the second the bullet struck him between the eyes. His body lay only ten yards away from her, still bleeding out.

Lexi located Hopper crouching behind a statue of what looked like a giant iguana. He was closer to the shooter than anybody and was yet to be spotted by Cog.

Norman still lay out in the open, hands over the back of his head and screaming. Cog turned his sights on him now, but didn't shoot. Instead he marched on over and dragged him onto his feet.

Cog placed the gun against Norman's head. "Everybody out where I can see them, now."

"Not going to happen," came Boss's reply.

"You come out or I blow his brains out."

Norman whimpered, tried to pull away but was quickly pulled back. The look on Cog's face was inhuman, his eyes swollen almost out of his head.

"What happened to you?" Lexi called out.

"The same thing that happened to everybody else."

"But you're still alive."

"No, I am as dead as all the rest. My body just does not yet know it. I was the first, chosen to watch those I infected turn to dust."

"Chosen by whom?"

Cog turned in Lexi's direction, tried to spot her. "Chosen by whoever sent the package. My only crime was being the one to open it, yet all have paid the price."

Boss shouted out. "You're a madman, Cog. Give yourself up and we can get you help."

"You can't cure death. Now come out or I will kill this man."

A tense silence took over.

Lexi made eye contact with Hopper, still undiscovered behind the iguana statue. He was inching out, trying to get an angle on Cog. He wanted Lexi to give him confirmation. She looked at Cog and saw that he was near the statue and facing slightly away. She gave Hopper the nod. Do it.

"Three seconds," Cog shouted.

Hopper gave Lexi one last look and stepped out from behind the statue, ready to make a move on Cog.

Something struck Lexi in the back and sent her sprawling out of the fire exit and out into the open. She spun around to see that Gellar was coming towards her with a snarl on her lips. She glanced sideways and saw Hopper rushing towards Cog, who was distracted by what was happening with Lexi.

But he was too slow.

Cog swung his arm and smashed Hopper in the face with the butt of his revolver, sending him to his knees in agony. Norman broke free and ran into cover beside Boss who threw him to the ground where he was safe.

Lexi still stood out in the open with Gellar stalking towards her.

Cog booted Hopper in the stomach sending him onto his back, incapacitated. Then raised his pistol.

But pointed it at Lexi.

Lexi had one eye on Gellar and one eye on the gun pointed at her. She felt her bladder loosen, but tried to keep calm. She started backing away from Gellar while putting her hands up where Cog could see them. "Please," she begged them both.

Gellar kept on coming, but Cog did not shoot her. Instead he let a feral grin find its way to his bulging, black lips. "Why waste the bullet?" He turned and ran away, laughing hysterically.

Gellar fell on top of Lexi and started to wrestle with her, just like the woman at the top of the Helter-skelter had.

"Lexi!" She heard her father shout out.

"Dad, help me."

Boss grabbed hold of Gellar's shoulder straps and began yanking her away from his daughter. The American woman was strong, but together they managed to pull her away. But she came right back at them relentlessly. Every time they hit her or shoved her away, Gellar came back for more. She was one of them now. One of the dead.

Lexi swallowed a lump in her throat as she looked at the dead American. She had liked Gellar, respected her bravery. But somehow that bite on her neck had infected her and now she was gone; just another monster.

"We need to put her down," Lexi said, surprising herself by how cold she sounded.

"We might be able to do something," Boss said.

Lexi shook her head. She picked the fire extinguisher she had dropped and walked towards Gellar. The woman snarled at her no sense or recognition. They weren't teammates anymore.

"I'm sorry, soldier," Lexi said, then smashed the fire extinguisher into the middle of Gellar's face. It took another two hits to drop her, but once Gellar fell onto her back, Lexi quickly straddled her and brought the fire extinguisher down on her face enough times to finish the job. By the time Gellar stopped moving, she had no face left.

Hopper let out a grown from nearby and climbed up onto his knees. Boss went over and helped him while Lexi slid off of Gellar and sat on the floor. Norman had broken cover, too, and quickly picked up his axe. Lexi gave him a stern look.

"Next time I say take cover, don't just flop on the ground where you're standing."

Norman looked upset. "I'm sorry. I really not like guns. Where I from, guns are very bad."

Lexi allowed herself to soften and nodded. Norman wasn't a solider and he had saved them all earlier. "I just don't want anyone else getting killed."

"How did that mofo get a gun anyway?" Hopper asked.

"I'm sure they keep a few locked up somewhere," Boss said. "Grand Galaxies has a massive security roster."

"For all the good it did," Hopper said. He clutched his ribs gingerly. His nose was bleeding. "Poor Trent, man."

Lexi went on over to where Trent lay in a pool of his own blood. Aside form the small red dot in his forehead, he looked his usual self. She let out a sigh and suddenly felt tears fill her eyes. "This is so screwed up. First Miller, now Gellar and Trent." She turned on her father. "What the fuck is wrong here? Why did SABA only send us to deal with a shitstorm this big?"

Boss grunted. The gunshot wound in his shoulder was only shallow and he seemed to be dealing with it via little more than a wince here and there. He'd been lucky. "I told you, Lexi. No body had any idea."

She didn't buy it. "Somebody targeted this place. SABA must have known that a terrorist act could have been behind the radio silence."

"They trusted us to report back if a bigger team was needed. My orders were to respond back if the situation was extreme."

Lexi shook her head. She had questions, but couldn't yet form them into words. Something was wrong here. There were too many things that made no sense.

"Why did your American friend turn into space zombie?" Norman asked.

Lexi looked at him like he was an idiot. "Because she was bitten by one. It's pretty obvious this this thing spreads easily. When Gellar got bitten she was infected."

"That make no sense," Norman said.

"It makes perfect sense," Hopper argued.

Norman was shaking his head adamantly. "No, no sense. Look." He rolled up his sleeve. "It make no sense because I bit twenty-four hour ago and I feel fine."

They all stared at the nasty-looking bite mark on Norman's arm and then looked at each other in confusion. Was the virus spreading some other way?

Hopper was the first to comment. "I'm convinced Gellar changed because she was bitten. There's no other way."

"She went near the meat in the cargo bay," Boss said.

"And I had my entire arm in it," Hopper rebutted. "I'm okay."

"Maybe I immune," Norman suggested.

No one said otherwise.

"Maybe you are," Lexi admitted.

"Or just damn lucky," Hopper said.

"No," Lexi said. "If luck played a part in the infection then there would be others who didn't turn."

"Maybe they not have place to hide like me," Norman said.

"Yeah, perhaps. But if you are immune, then we need to get you back to Earth alive. If this virus ever gets released at home, you might hold the key to a cure."

Norman propped his axe over his shoulder and smiled wearily. "If my blood make you all want to protect me, then that fine with me."

Hopper looked down at Trent and said, "I wouldn't get too excited. So far we've sucked pretty bad at keeping people breathing."

Lexi hated that he was right, but wasn't ready to quit just yet. "All the more reason to get our arses to the comms room," she said, "and then get the hell out of here."

"Okay, then," Boss said. "Let's keep going."

-10-

They headed inside the Mexican restaurant and headed straight for the staff corridor at the back. The only problem was that the restaurant wasn't empty. There was a dead employee wandering about, still dressed in his apron and red company baseball cap.

Norman was far more comfortable dealing with the dead than he was when faced with a gun, and he trotted forward now and swung his axe like a baseball bat. It lodged halfway through the dead employee's neck, but it did the job. The dead man hit the floor and stopped moving.

"You're disturbingly good at that," Hopper said.

Norman pulled his axe free and shrugged. "Learn fast or die."

"Good point."

They made it into the corridor and found that the back of the building stretched much further back than it appeared from the outside. The first offices pertained to the restaurant, but further back they began to concern themselves with the administration of the park at large. The accountancy department and training centre lay nearby but were of no interest. What was of interest was the flight of stairs below a sign reading: SECURITY OFFICES & COMMUNICATIONS SUITE.

"We made it," Hopper said with a relieved sigh.

"We don't know what we'll find yet," Lexi said. "That maniac, Cog, is still around somewhere."

"We'll deal with him," Boss said flatly and then took the first step.

The staircase went up a single story and deposited them in an upper foyer. Hopper immediately went on over to a bank of vending machines next to a seating area. None of them carried cash so he made a ruckus by smashing in the glass with the padded elbow of his suit.

Boss hissed. "Do you have to do everything so bloody loud?"

Hopper pulled out a packet of potato crisps and started munching on them. When he spoke he spat crumbs everywhere. "Sorry, Boss."

Boss shook his head irritably. "Let's just end this."

Lexi frowned. End this? Far as she saw it, getting to the comms room was only halfway. Even if they hailed for rescue, the military ships would take at least eight hours to arrive from Earth. There was still the question of twenty thousand missing guests. Where the hell were they all?

The biggest area ahead was the security galley. Three separate doors along one wall led to it. The communications suite, however, was right at the far end of the foyer and accessed only by a single door. They headed there now.

Boss waited for everybody to assemble then put a finger to his lips to hush them all.

Then they went inside.

Lexi had expected to find Cog pointing a gun at them, but the only thing moving were the screen savers on the various monitors.

"Can we still do what we need to without Trent?" Lexi asked.

"I know my way around," Hopper said. "I'll do what I can."

"Get to it then," Boss ordered, a little unkindly.

Hopper plonked down on one of the seats and wheeled

himself towards the main console. Immediately he started typing away and clicking on the mouse. While he was busy, Lexi stayed near the door, making sure the foyer remained clear. Last thing they needed was a horde of dead people trapping them inside the cramped communications suite.

She couldn't believe that she was still alive after two marines and a tech specialist were dead. She was just a navigator; the only danger she was supposed to encounter was carpal tunnel syndrome and bad posture.

"Shit! Damn damn damn."

Lexi spun around to see Hopper slamming his fist down on the desk.

"What is it?" Boss asked.

Hopper swivelled on his chair so that he was facing them. "Somebody's disabled the conduit."

Boss frowned. "Explain."

"The conduit is a bunch of cables leading from the comms centre to the dish outside. Without being connected to the satellite array, we can't send a message further than a couple of miles."

"What do you mean it's disabled?" Lexi asked.

"I mean somebody has cut it or dismantled it in some way. Every time I try to connect, it fails. I can't get a single packet through and there's nothing I can do on the system to remedy it. It's not software related. Somebody has been messing with the hardware."

Norman placed the head of his axe down on the ground and flopped all of his weight onto the handle. "Oh brother. We never get out of here, do we?"

Boss rubbed at the stubble on his chin. "Can we fix the conduit, Hopper?"

"Depends on what's been done to it. We're better off making straight for the array itself. I can tap into it and send a message directly. It'll have to be basic, but someone should get it on Earth and understand we need help."

"Where's the array?" Lexi asked.

Hopper leant back in his chair and sighed. "At the top of the Astronomer's Finger."

Lexi groaned. "You mean that huge, massive tower we passed on the way in?"

"It is big," Norman said. "I go shopping there yesterday. They have biggest Burger Queen."

Hopper sniffed and then nodded. "I could eat."

"What about the jamming signal?" Boss asked. "Is that still in place?"

"Yeah. It's not coming from anything in here. What's strange is that it's localised."

Lexi crossed her arms. "What do you mean?"

"I mean that the Hermes was disabled, but that giant ass spider that jumped at you was working just fine. The jamming signal seems targeted, but the only way I know for something like that to be possible is if the signal is shortwave."

"What are you getting at?" Boss said irritably. He'd been getting les and less patient for the last few hours.

"I think Grand Galaxies is fitted with localised signal jammers, as in separate units attached to each section of the installation that can be controlled individually."

"Wait," Lexi said. "That would mean..."

"That this place is fitted with signal jammers as standard. No one sabotaged this place, they just made use of the systems already in place."

Norman was looking utterly confused. "But why? Why would a tourist facility have signal jammers installed?"

"A very good question," Lexi said. "Cog said this place has a hidden agenda. I'm starting to believe him."

"Nonsense," her father said. "We've already discussed this place's need to contain communications should the need arise."

Hopper scoffed. "Well, everyone here seems to be dead, and thanks to the signal jammers, not a soul could get a phone call through to their loved ones. Whoever built this place is a tool."

"The British and American Governments built this place. The administration we all work for."

"So what we do then?" Norman asked. "We make it here, but it is complete shit party."

Hopper grinned. "Not a complete shit party."

Lexi looked at him. "No?"

"Nope. There's an armoury inside the Security vestibule. I've just unlocked it. Time to arm up."

"Best suggestion anybody's had all day," Lexi said. "Let's be quick about it."

They left the communications suite and headed back along the foyer to the first of the three doors leading to the security area. When they moved inside, they were met by an endless bank of television monitors, each one showing a different angle of the park or surrounding facilities.

"Whoa," Hopper said. "There's not an inch of this place not on camera."

"That's good," Lexi said. "Maybe we can find out where Cog is, as well as all the other guests."

"Let's find the armoury first," Hopper said. "I'll feel much better with something thick and powerful in my hands."

Lexi huffed. "Typical man."

They moved carefully through the vestibule, mindful of being ambushed from the dark corners behind the many desks and computers. They found another room on their left. Its door was hanging ajar, the electronic keypad beside it lit a solid green. ENTER.

"Open sesame," Hopper said, grabbing the door and pulling it ajar.

"You're frikkin' kidding me," Lexi said as she stepped inside and looked around. The armoury was twenty feet wide and lined with rows upon rows of low velocity assault rifles and handguns. There was a huge crate in the centre of the room packed with ball bearing rounds reading for loading into magazines. "Why the hell would a theme park need this kind of fire power?" she asked. "There's enough here to equip an army."

"It's not our business," Boss said. "Let's just take what we need and do what needs doing."

Lexi rolled her eyes. She was starting to get pissed off with her father, and she only gave him a break because he was their squad leader and they'd lost three members of the team. It probably weighed down on him hard. He wasn't performing at his best.

Hopper was the first to grab a rifle, and he also slipped a handgun into his belt. He located the cache of magazines and started filling them up with ball bearings from the crate. "Anybody know how much these things hold?" he asked.

"Just keep filling till they're full," Lexi said, grabbing a rifle for herself and joining him at the crate. She was halfway through filling up the first magazine when they heard something from the back of the room. It came from a stack of shelving filled with riot helmets. One of the helmets fell off onto the floor.

"There's someone behind there," Hopper said, jamming in his magazine and flicking off the safety.

Boss put a hand up to stay any action and took a step towards the shelf. He spoke with authority. "I am Commander Sharman and this is a rescue operation. If you need assistance, please identify yourself and step out where we can see you."

There was another jolt. Another helmet slipped from the shelf and fell to the ground.

"Reveal yourself," Boss demanded.

Lexi went back to filling her magazine with ball bearings. She had a bad feeling.

Hopper stayed where he was, aiming his rifle ahead and looking eager to pull the trigger.

Somebody stepped out from behind the shelving unit. They were followed by two more bodies. Then another half-dozen.

Lexi stopped filling her magazine and shoved it into the base of her rifle, only half full. "Shit!"

The dead people numbered nearly ten, and they all approached, hands outstretched, teeth grinding.

Hopper let rip, aiming high. His first few rounds struck the ceiling but he brought the stream of ball bearings down onto the crowd. The first dead man's head exploded into mush. The second dead man was dealt with easily, too. But then came the problem.

Hopper kept his finger on the trigger, but the ball bearings ricocheted off the riot helmets impotently, hitting the ceiling or smashing the overhead lights.

"They're wearing armour," Lexi shouted.

The dead security guards were togged in full body armour and riot helmets. They had obviously been readying themselves for battle when they were infected.

Lexi raised her rifle and joined the fight. She aimed low, trying to hit the unarmoured legs of her targets. Shinbones and kneecaps shattered. A couple of dead security guards crumpled onto their fronts, but they continued forwards, crawling on their bellies.

"Retreat," Boss bellowed.

Hopper refused. He stood his ground and kept firing. Eventually Boss had to grab him and pull him back. "Move it!"

"We need these weapons," Hopper screamed.

"Not if it ends up killing us." Boss dragged him roughly into the corridor. Lexi shoved the armoury door closed behind them, but couldn't lock it. The catch was electronic and Hopper had overridden it.

The dead men pushed against the other side, pushing it open again.

Norman ran up to help Lexi and together they fought to keep the door closed. But they quickly begun losing ground, their feet slipping on the tiled floor.

"Damn it," Lexi said. "We need to run for it."

Norman shook his head. "Big shits."

"Now, let go now."

She and Norman released the door at the same time. They turned and sprinted, while the door exploded open and the dead men fell through. They gave chase, seeming to gather speed as their joints loosened up.

Boss led the retreat and even Hopper was committed to fleeing now. He held his rifle closely against his chest but was cursing loudly. "I'm almost empty," he said. "The magazine barely lasts a few seconds."

"It does when you keep your finger on the trigger," Lexi said.

"How was I supposed to know? I'm not a goddamn soldier. We needed those other rifles."

"It's in the past now. Forget it."

They reached the staircase that had led them from the Mexican Restaurant below. The dead men were sprinting now. Lexi was panting, not sure how much longer she could run. Hopper seemed to sense this and bought them some time. He let off the last of his rounds and took out the legs of the two nearest runners. They flopped on the ground and tripped up their colleagues, leaving a pile of scrambling bodies on the floor.

Hopper nodded at her and they got running again, joining Norman and Boss at the bottom of the stairs. They wasted no time and kept on running until they were out of the Mexican restaurant and back outside in the park.

"How do we get to the tower?" Lexi asked.

Norman pointed. "That way. Through Ice Lands."

"My rifle is empty. You're the only one still packing heat." Hopper meant Lexi who she still held a loaded rifle.

"Do you want my magazine?" she asked. "I feel kind of stupid holding this thing anyway."

Hopper shook his head. "Your turn to be the hero."

They got moving quickly, cutting a path through the deserted Forbidden Zone. Lexi wondered if it was the same direction Cog had fled and was pretty sure it was. How long before they ran into him again? It must have been he who had damaged the conduit.

The sands of the Forbidden Zone began to ease and eventually turned into pretend ice sheets and glaciers. Lexi and the others headed through an archway and entered the Ice Lands. Like the other sectors, it resembled the surface of a hostile planet, but this time it was a little more child-friendly, with fluffy creatures resembling penguins and the extinct polar bears of Earth. The rides, also, were much gentler. A monorail ran overhead, disappearing up a fake mountain, and just ahead was a carousel with ride-on sledges. Ice cream was available from a nearby store shaped like an igloo.

"We keep going," Norman said. "It is at very end of this sector."

Hopper was still carrying his empty rifle but held it by rail on the top, more like a briefcase now than a weapon. "When you were hiding out, Norman; did you see where all of the infected guests went?"

"They all huddle together in great big mess, but I not see where they go."

Hopper sighed. "Great. Let's hope we don't get to find out."

-11-

The Ice Lands section was not as large as the others and they managed to traverse it in a little over ten minutes. No one had spoken along the way, too tense to concentrate on anything other than keeping watch for threats. Lexi led with her rifle but her father kept himself only a single step behind her. He seemed to have calmed a little, his shoulders lower and more relaxed, but he still wasn't the reassuring leader he was well known to be.

Norman pointed the way, even though it was obvious. They were approaching a large mountain that seemed to stretch up forever but was actually painted in such a way as only to appear so. The top of the mountain was actually just wall and ceiling. Directly ahead was a large cave entrance, but it was really just a set of double doors leading out into the next area. A wooden sign was scrawled with the woods: Here there be shopping.

When they passed through, they found themselves in a non-themed area. Lexi felt like she was back to reality, away from the make-believe theme park and surrounded by glass shop fronts and marble fountains. There was an escalator leading upwards and they took it. The upper floors were walled with glass and the vastness of space encircled them, whilst below was the domed roof of the Grand Galaxy amusement park.

"This is amazing," Hopper said.

"It quickly get boring," Norman said. "I was here for hours with Suzie from Sales."

Lexi looked at Norman to see whether or not he was sad. He didn't seem to be. "Was Suzie a friend?"

"Not really, but we hit off when we queue at London Terminal. We were on date, but all I end up doing was holding all of Suzie's bags."

Hopper chuckled. "Sounds about right. Women, right."

"Amen to that, brother."

"You're sorry she's dead though, right?" Lexi asked.

Norman shrugged. "Lot of people dead. I kind of numb to it at this point."

Lexi frowned. She wasn't sure she ever wanted to be numb to people dying, but then she hadn't lived through what Norman had. Maybe his reaction was understandable.

The floors seemed to climb forever and before long the surface of the moon stretched on for hundreds of miles in all directions. Suddenly Lexi felt extremely small and insignificant.

Hopper pointed upwards at the glass windows. "Look."

Lexi looked up and saw a beautiful sight. "Earth."

She'd seen it a dozen times before from space, but seeing it now took her breath away. It was beautiful. It was home. Perhaps she wasn't so jaded after all.

"Let's hope we get back to it soon," she said, wheeling towards the next set of stairs. It led to the final floor, so far as shopping and eating areas went.

Hopper spun around slowly, checking things out. "The satellite array is at the very top of the tower. There must be another staircase somewhere."

The floor was entirely made up of restaurants and each of them was backed by a panoramic glass window. There seemed no obvious route upwards.

But then Lexi saw a possibility. "I think that's it. That door."

Between an Italian eatery and a place that seemed to specialise in snails was an unassuming blue, wooden door. It led to neither restaurant on either side.

"Good spot," Hopper said, rushing over to the door. He ran his hands over it but failed to find a handle. There was, however, a keyhole.

They grouped together behind Hopper.

Lexi said. "Looks like it opens outwards."

Hopper shoved on the door. "It seems pretty thick. Might end up being a broom closet, but I think we need to get it open to see."

"I agree," Boss said, the first time he had said anything in a while.

"How, though?" Lexi asked. "I wouldn't even want to think about who has the key."

"I have key," Norman said. They all looked at him as he propped his axe on his shoulder.

Boss grunted affirmatively. "Hop to it then, civilian."

Norman rushed forward and swung the axe, burying it in the centre of the door where it wedged. He put his foot against the wood and levered it free again. The next blow he aimed right at the lock. It bent. He hit it three more times and was sweating by the time the door shunted open.

Boss nodded at the civilian. "Good work."

Lexi put a hand against the door and glanced at her father. "Are we ready?"

He nodded.

Lexi pushed open the door.

All was quiet. At first.

The door did indeed lead to a staircase, utilitarian and unlike the posh marble steps of the previous flights. This one was not meant to be seen by public eyes. As soon as Lexi placed her foot on the very first step, a figure appeared at the top. It ran towards her immediately.

Lexi backed up and raised her rifle.

It was no man that leapt through the door at her, but another one of the humanoids.

"YOU HAVE ATTEMPTED TO ENTER A RESTRICTED AREA," it squawked at them.

"Stand down, steel-cheeks," Hopper said. "We have full authorisations to be here."

The humanoid glanced at Hopper, its eyes pulsing blue. ""YOU ARE UNDER ARREST. SIT DOWN ON THE FLOOR AND CROSS YOUR LEGS UNTIL A MEMBER OF SECURITY CAN ARRIVE TO DETAIN YOU."

"Bite me."

The humanoid turned to face Lexi, who in turn faced it with her rifle slung high. "DROP YOUR WEAPON OR LETHAL FORCE WILL BE EXERCISED."

Lexi swallowed, unsure what to do. She looked at her father.

Boss was not happy and the irritation was clear in his voice as he told her to, "Shoot the thing to pieces."

Lexi pulled the trigger.

She was not a soldier and her training with assault rifles was non-existent. The weapon bucked in her hands and punched her shoulder like a fist, but she fought to control it and aimed a continuous stream of ball bearings directly into the humanoid's chest.

The humanoid stumbled backwards, sparks and torn shreds of latex skin filling the air in a cloud. But once the initial impact dissipated, the machine swiped its arm, rebalanced, and stalked towards Lexi again.

She kept firing, ripping an ever-widening hole in the humanoid's chest. But it kept on coming. She started taking steps backwards, keeping a distance between her and the machine.

"Aim for the head," Hopper shouted.

Lexi caught his eye and nodded. She refocused and aimed for the head. It was a tougher target to hit, and she missed with half of the rounds she fired, but the ball bearings eventually hit the target and caused massive damage. Sparks and black lubricant began leaking all over the place.

Click!

Lexi released the trigger and pulled it again, but nothing happened except that same harrowing click. Her rifle was dry. And the humanoid was not yet done. "I'm out of ammo," she whimpered.

Hopper ran forwards to help, but the humanoid shot out an arm and swatted him to the ground like a fly. Boss moved himself between his daughter and the machine but didn't seem to know what to do.

The humanoid stalked them. One of its blue eyes was shattered and sparking, and its lower jaw was hanging loose by a single wire, but it had lost none of its murderous intent.

Boss grabbed the rifle from Lexi and swung it by the barrel, bludgeoning the humanoid with the stock end. Its head rocked backwards on its shoulder, but quickly sprang back. It snatched the rifle from Boss and quickly snapped it in half.

"YOU ARE GUILTY OF VANDALISING THE PROPERTY OF GRAND GALAXY ENTERTAIMENT RESORT. YOU ARE UNDER ARREST." The machine's warning was even more foreboding seeing as it no longer had a mouth with which to speak. It grabbed Boss by the shoulder, gripping him where he had earlier been shot. He screamed out in a high-pitched tone.

Lexi looked around for a solution and saw Norman standing there, holding his axe, but he was frozen to the spot.

"Norman, help us!"

He still didn't move.

The humanoid continued squeezing Boss's shoulder and forced him down to his knees. "UNDER SECTION 971, LETHAL FORCE HAS NOW BEEN AUTHORISED."

Lexi shouted at Norman again, but still the man did nothing. His wide eyes were fixed on the humanoid. His lower lip quivered.

"Lexi, get out of here," Boss managed to bellow at her.

"I won't leave you."

"Give me that!" Lexi looked around to see Hopper shoving Norman away and snatching the man's axe from him. With it, he raced towards the humanoid, span a full circle, then swung the axe horizontally and lopped off its head. It hit the ground like a football and rolled away, while the dismembered body slumped to its knees where it remained like it was praying. Boss got up off the ground, clutching his bleeding shoulder, and kicked the machine over onto its back. "Back to the scrap yard for you," he said.

Lexi grabbed her father and held him steady. Blood leaked down his chest from the aggravated wound on his shoulder, but no real additional damage had been done.

Hopper, too, was hurt, rubbing his hip and wincing. "Those things hit harder than a tax bill," he muttered.

Lexi went up to Norman and shoved him. "What the hell were you doing?"

"I...sorry."

"That's not good enough."

"Yeah," Hopper chimed in. "You're like a regular gangster when it comes to killing zombies, but anything else and you freeze like a popsicle."

"I...I... The dead do not scare me."

"They sure as hell scare me," Hopper said.

"They don't scare me because they already bite me and I fine. In fact, they not even interested in me."

Lexi frowned. "What?"

Norman took a large gulp. He was covered in sweat and extremely pasty. He looked as much a coward as he had just behaved. "After I got bite on my arm, the space zombies lose interest. I able to walk right by them."

"But when we found you, you were hiding," Lexi said.

Norman nodded. "Still survivors hang around for while. They a little... out of mind, yes? I think better to just low-lie until help arrive."

Hopper wore a disgusted look. "This whole time, you've been immune and unmolested by those things, but you've still allowed us to take all the risks. You could have scoped things out for us without any risk to yourself. You're a coward, man."

"No," he said. "I not coward. They still risks. They are other survivors, like one who kill Trent. And bad machines. Who know how long dead men ignore me. Eventually, luck will run out. Give back my axe."

Hopper held the axe up and seemed like he was about to hand it over, but then he lowered it and shook his head. "Think it's of more use to me. I don't have a get out of jail free card like you. Plus, I'm willing to actually use it when it counts."

"I save you all," Norman said.

"Yeah, you did," Lexi said. "Which is why we're not kicking your butt right now."

"Enough," Boss shouted, recovered enough to stand tall again. "Let's get up those bloody stairs and begin sorting this mess out."

They took the staircase in single file as it was too narrow to do otherwise. The only weapon they had now was Hopper's axe, so he led the way. The stairs did not lead directly to another floor, but instead twisted and turned back and forth, climbing ever higher. Bare cement walls, not the glass facades of the public areas, surrounded the stairwell and made the journey extremely bleak.

By the time they reached a doorway, they were all out of breath. Norman most of all, for he had to kneel down on the steps and take a rest before they went on. No one argued, for they could all do with a quick breather.

"You okay?" Lexi asked Hopper. The bridge of his nose was swollen and his eyes were dark.

"I used to take worse beatings from my father so, yeah, I'm good."

Lexi raised her eyebrows. "Are you being serious? That's horrible."

Hopper shrugged. "Made me what I am today. I joined the corps to leave my past behind. I worked my arse off and made sure I was the best, so that I never had to feel worthless ever again."

Lexi didn't say that she was sorry, for she knew that Hopper did not require pity, so she just patted him on the back. She looked at her own father and thought about how much better off she had been. Boss had never been a devoted father, his passion lay with the corps, but he at least had loved her and had never hit her. She couldn't imagine what it would be like if he ever had. She reached out to touch Hopper again, but he had moved away towards the door.

Eventually Norman made it back to his feet, despite still looking grim. Boss got the nod from everybody and they prepared to continue the mission. The mission that started bad and had only got worse.

"Maybe Norman should open the door this time," Hopper said. "Seeing as how he's Mr Invisible to the dead guests."

Norman didn't argue. He made his way to the front of the group and reached for the door handle. To everybody's surprise, it was unlocked. They all stepped through and found themselves inside an oily work area. Machine parts and benches filled the bare floor and the overhead strip lights flickered with ongoing vibrations. One of the benches held a humanoid with no arms and only one leg."

"This looks like some sort of repair area," Lexi said.

"It takes a lot to keep a satellite array running," Hopper said. "They probably have a team of engineers stationed here. Wonder why there's nobody here now. You'd think it would be nice and safe up here."

"Maybe we'll find someone," Lexi said. "Fingers crossed."

Norman went over to one of the benches and picked up a wrench. Lexi did him one better and discovered a welding torch. She gave it a quick blast to test it out and an immense blue flame shot out of the nozzle, making her flinch.

Hopper held his axe and grinned. "Now you're really smoking."

Lexi groaned. "You're like a character out of a bad book."

He frowned at her. "A book? Nobody reads anymore."

"I'm not nobody."

"We must be near the top now," Boss said. "The array should be within reach. Let's find it."

"Let's try over there." Hopper pointed. "I think I see something."

It turned out that Hopper could see something. Bodies. A lot of them.

-12-

"Who are all these people?" Lexi asked. "They look like guests."

She knelt down beside the body of a young girl. She was wearing a hoodie with The Driller printed on it and bright pink tennis pumps. She was definitely a guest. A bullet hole dotted her chest right below her neck. Upon closer inspection, Lexi saw entry wounds on all of the bodies.

"Somebody killed these people," Hopper said, reaching the same conclusion that she had.

"Looks like they were all shot in the chest," Boss said. "Whoever shot them knew what they were doing."

Norman doubled over and vomited. It was a strange reaction seeing as he'd been surrounded by walking corpses for more than twenty-four hours and had dismembered several of them with his axe.

"You okay?" Lexi asked him.

Norman wiped his mouth. "Fine. I think everything is just getting to me."

Hopper nodded. "Understandable."

"I don't understand," Lexi said, turning her attention back to the several dozen dead park guests. "How did they end up here and why would somebody shoot them?"

"Perhaps they were infected," Hopper said.

"No. If they were infected they would have come back, wouldn't they? None of these people were shot in the head. I think they were healthy. They were survivors."

Hopper grimaced. "Why would somebody want to shoot survivors? You think it was Cog?"

"I don't know. Cog had a revolver when we saw him last. I don't think he could have taken down so many people on his own."

"Then who?"

Boss cleared his throat. "It doesn't matter. We can't save the dead."

A noise caught their attention.

Hopper grabbed a tight hold on his axe and stepped towards the source. Lexi backed him up with her welding torch. Norman stayed back with his wrench.

"Who's there?" Boss shouted.

"Captain Yanniger," came the accented reply.

"Are you armed?"

From behind a group of fuel barrels, a handgun skittered across the floor and came to rest out in the open. "Not anymore."

Cautiously, they spread out and approached the group of barrels. Despite having no weapon of any kind, Boss took point. He seemed unconcerned by any threat and strode purposely, fearlessly.

Together they rounded the barrels and found a man sitting up against the wall. He was wearing full body armour like the dead men they had encountered inside the armoury. He was also bleeding from a ragged wound on his neck.

Lexi knelt beside the man immediately, went to place a hand against his wound and apply pressure, but he swatted her away urgently. "No," he said. "I've been bitten. Don't get my blood on you."

Lexi pulled her hand away. "Do you know about the virus?"

He nodded. "It was engineered by the League of Joa."

Lexi frowned. "Those fundamentalists operating out of Israel? Nobody takes them seriously, not even Israel."

The man swallowed and it obviously caused him pain as it took him a while to find his voice again. "European Intelligence has known Joa have been working on a biological weapon for years. They finally perfected it and sent it here."

Hopper crossed his arms. "Why attack an amusement park?"

"As a threat. To show the world what the virus will do if released on Earth. This is their Hiroshima – a warning to their enemies."

Lexi hissed. "Show people what the virus can do without risking it getting out of control on Earth; clever. They'll be able to demand anything now. But wait," she looked down at the wounded captain, "how the hell do you know all this? You're just a security guard for an amusement park."

He laughed and it hurt him. He winced and held his neck. "If you think this place is just an amusement park, you're an idiot. The League of Joa targeted here for a reason. This place is a military asset. I'm not a guard. I'm United States Inteligence."

"What are you talking about?" Hopper said.

"Nothing. I'm done talking about it. You'll find out soon enough. Just do me a favour and kill me. I don't want to become one of those things."

"You're turning?" Lexi said. "Where is the person who bit you, and what happened to all of those guests back there?"

"Orders."

"You killed them all."

"Not me. My men. One of the guards who worked on this level allowed them in for safety, but this place is not for the public. They had to be dealt with."

"Where are you're men now?" Boss asked.

"Dead. Like me."

Lexi kicked the man, suddenly enraged. "Tell me what's going on here," she screamed. "Was it you who jammed communications? Sabotaged our ship?"

There was more noise ahead and Lexi stepped away from the Captain to look around.

"Oh, hell," Hopper muttered.

The captain's men had arrived, and every one of them was dead.

The captain let out a moan, but was still alive. "My gun," he said. "Grab my gun."

Lexi spotted the handgun on the floor and quickly snatched it up. She estimated five dead guards in total and fired at the closest without even blinking. The round took the dead guard between the eyes and dropped him cold. She re-sighted her aim and took out the next and the next, but the final two wore riot helmets.

Hopper took the first of the two remaining dead men. He swung his axe like a golf club and shattered the knee of his target. Once the guard tumbled down onto its belly, he kicked the helmet off of its head and brought the axe down hard.

That left just one more guard.

Norman stepped up. "Let me. He not hurt me."

They all stood back while Norman took charge. He strolled casually up to the dead man and grabbed its riot helmet with both hands. As expected, the guard simply tried to push past Norman and get to the rest of them. Norman removed the helmet and tossed it to the floor. Then he bought the wrench up over his head and smashed it down on the dead man's skull.

Five bodies lay on the ground, the threat dealt with.

"We're getting better at this," Hopper said. "Does that worry anybody else?"

"What do we do with him?" Lexi asked, motioning towards the fading captain.

"Kill him," Boss said.

Lexi looked at her father and frowned. "What?"

"He's already dead. Do him a favour."

Lexi looked at the gun in her hand and then shook her head. "I'm not just going to shoot him."

"I don't mind," the captain said, waving an arm from where he still sat on the ground. "Shoot me, please."

Lexi stood firm. In fact, she strode up to her father and shoved the gun at him. "Shoot him yourself."

Her father snatched the gun out of her hands and shot the captain in the chest. The man wheezed for a second, then died. Boss followed up the shot with a second straight to the head. He shoved the gun back at his daughter and marched away.

Lexi looked down at the gun and saw her hands tremble. Hooper came over to her and gently prised it away from her. "Maybe I should take this," he said.

They exchanged glances for a moment and then followed after Boss. Neither said it, but they were both upset by what they had just witnessed. Norman hurried from behind to keep up with them, and he didn't look any more confident than they did.

-13-

"This is it," Hopper said, with more than a little relief in his voice. "This is the satellite array."

Lexi looked around at the room they were in and was impressed. The ceiling was glass plated, allowing them to look directly up into the stars. It also allowed them to see the monolithic dish outside and the many smaller dishes mounted around it. In front of them was a massive bank of computers.

Hopper hurried over and begun accessing the systems. He used the comms unit on his forearm that they all wore. SABA had uploaded to them all the authorisations they needed, but that didn't stop Hopper from cursing a few times as he struggled to get to grips with the firewalls.

"Do you need help?" Lexi asked him.

"I need Trent, but you'll do, I suppose."

Lexi tutted, but didn't take offence. She joined him at the console and leant forward. "What am I looking at?"

"I'm trying to get into the communication hub. I should be able to send out a simple message and get a response, but it seems like some sort of override has been put in place. It was done on top of the regular operating system so it's not much interested in my administrator rights."

"What do you mean?"

"I mean that somebody stuck a firewall of their own in place. I can't send a message without taking it down."

"Maybe it was the captain." Lexi scowled at her father. "Too bad he's dead."

"He wouldn't have been of any use," Boss said. "Why would he lock us out of the system and then tell us how to get back in?"

Lexi ignored him, placed a hand on Hopper's shoulder. "Can you do anything?"

"I'm not sure. Let me try a back door. I'll see if any of the other systems have native control over the satellite. I may be able to... wow, wait a minute. What the...?"

"What?" Boss asked. "What have you found, Hopper?"

Hopper turned around to face Boss. There was a look of utter confusion on his face. "I just accessed a sub-directory called Orbital Assault Platform."

Lexi baulked. "What? Assault? You mean Grand Galaxy was built with weapon systems?"

"Not just weapons systems," Hopper explained. "Orbital weapons. As in weapons pointed at space, or even Earth."

Norman bent over and fell into a chair. He slumped forwards and began panting. "This supposed to be nice vacation they say. Very relaxing, very nice they tell me. Bullshits."

Everyone ignored him. Lexi looked at Boss to see what he thought about the situation, but he didn't seem shocked or angry like she was.

"Oh, God," she said, reading her father's expression like a book. "You knew about this, didn't you?"

Boss sighed and took a seat. He rubbed at his chin for a few moments and then looked at his daughter with tired, suddenly very old eyes. "Yes, I knew. That's why we're here. When the American and British governments built this place, they couldn't condone such a monumental cost for a commercial project alone. It's been ten years and this place has only just turned a profit. That's beside the point, though, because this it was never intended to be a getaway for those rich enough to afford it. It's a weapon, Lexi. It's the greatest weapon ever built. From this station, our government can target a bird in its nest in any country in the world. It has a link up to every allied satellite in space and can spy on every inch of the cosmos. It has saved millions of lives, by taking out the bad men before they even know they're on our radar."

"Including the League of Joa," Hopper said.

Boss nodded. "Their leader was assassinated several years ago. Somehow, they must have discovered the existence of this place and focused all of their attention on bringing it down."

"Game set and match to them," Hopper said.

"Why are we here?" Lexi asked. "What's our real mission?"

"The real mission was something only Gellar, Miller, and I, truly understood. We were to secure this place without any witnesses to what is really here, or..."

"Or what, goddamnit?"

"Or, if the facility is irredeemably compromised, the mission is to destroy it."

Lexi was so stunned that she fell back like a punch had hit her. "D-Destroy it how?"

"By turning the orbital blasters inwards."

Hopper picked up a chair and threw it. Everyone stared at him in surprise, but he just shrugged his shoulders. "Felt like a throw a chair moment."

Norman started coughing. When he caught his breath, he made a comment on the situation. "We can't die here. You have to get me back to Earth, remember? If this thing gets out back home then my blood might be cure. I'm immune."

Lexi was about to agree, but when she looked at him she found herself thinking something else. "I don't think that you are immune."

Norman frowned at her. "What? I was bitten a day and a half ago and I have not turned."

"Not yet, but I think you're going to. At first, I believed you were immune, but now you look like shit."

He sneered. "Thank you."

"No, she's right," Hopper said. "You look like a bear shit you out. You're ill, man."

"I feel fine."

Lexi looked at Norman and raised her eyebrows. "Really?"

"Okay, no. I feel like the death that is warmed up, but is just stress of situation. I not infected. I am immune."

Lexi shook her head, now completely sure. "I think you're resistant, but not immune. You're dying Norman. I'm sorry. The virus is in you, but for some reason your body fights it better than most. The virus is still going to win in the end, though."

Norman got up and waved his arms. "Immune, resistant, whatever. You still need me for tests and experiments and-"

"You'll never make it back to Earth," Boss said, his stern voice making everyone take a step back. "In fact, taking you to Earth would be a bloody awful idea. You're infectious."

"No!"

"Yes. This entire facility is now a hazard to life itself back on Earth. It has to be destroyed."

Norman was trembling with panic. His eyes had begun to bulge and were a fiery red at the edges. He took a step towards Boss, his arm extended threateningly.

There was a loud bang and Norman's head half-exploded. Hopper stood with his own arm extended, the captain's handgun now smoking from its muzzle.

Lexi gasped at him. "Damn it, Hopper. Not you, now? Why are we shooting people?"

"Because he was going to become a space chomper. He wasn't the type to quietly suffer – he would have become a hindrance – and we can't afford anything holding us back, Lexi, because we are getting of this goddamn lump of rock."

Boss frowned. "Impossible. We need to destroy this place."

"Yeah, you do that, Boss. You can stay right here and arm the systems; just as soon as me and your daughter get back in the Hermes and fly away."

"The Hermes is down," Lexi said.

"Only because of the jamming in that sector. I'm pretty sure I can release it. If your father stays behind, he can make sure no one interferes once we head back."

"No way, I'm not going to leave my father here to die."

"Yes, you are." Boss was speaking so they both shut up. "We can't get a message out because of the bloody communications override, but you two can get back to Earth and warn SABA and the goddamn Pentagon of what the League of Joa is capable of. They need to be warned. Hopper, do it."

Hopper raced over to the console and began tapping away.

"That madman, Cog, is still out there somewhere," Boss warned. "So be careful. Somebody has to stay here to make sure this place is turned to dust. You can either be here when that happens, or on your way home."

"No, this is crazy," but as Lexi said it, she knew there was no other way. The death and evilness in this place would devastate the Earth if it got free. There were far more lives at stake than just her father's, and he was going to do what he intended to do with or without her.

Hopper stood away from the console and nodded at them both. "It's done. The departure lounge and airlock is all systems go again. The Hermes should be back online."

Boss grunted. "Then it's decided."

Lexi sprang forward and threw her arms around her father. "I love you, dad."

"I love you too, sweetheart. I'm sorry I dragged you up here. I honestly never thought... I was told only to assemble a squad I trusted and who could keep a secret. I thought of you, but if I'd know..."

"It's okay."

"It's only okay as long as you get back to Earth."

"I'll get her home," Hopper said confidently.

"Good, now get out of here before I blow this place up with you in it."

Hopper holstered his gun and saluted. Lexi decided to do so, too. "It's been a pleasure, Commander," she said.

"Dismissed, Lieutenant."

Lexi smiled at her father for the very last time and left.

-14-

The journey down the multiple floors of the Astronomer's Finger was much easier than the one up it, but it still left each of them out of breath by the time they reached the bottom. Hopper sat Lexi down on a bench and went to go fetch her a drink from a nearby snack bar. The exhaustion didn't come only from her muscles and bones, but from her mind, too. She had witnessed hundreds of deaths, and knew that the actual number totalled thousands, but now she had just left her father to commit suicide. Her mind was being pulled in a dozen different directions and each and every yank threatened to snap her psyche in two.

Hopper returned with two coffees. It was steaming hot and the smell instantly brought back Lexi's focus.

"The machine was still on," Hopper said. "I literally could not ask for anything better right now."

Lexi took a sip of the hot beverage and burned her lips, but didn't care. She exhaled with pleasure. "Wow, I needed that."

"You okay?" he said. "I mean, considering..."

She nodded. "It is what it is. We have to get out of here. I'll save any breakdowns for back on Earth. This isn't the place."

"Your father is a hero."

"No, he's not. Placing weapons at Grand Galaxies put every single guest here at risk, and he knew that. We should be moving past all this bullshit. It's almost the 22nd Century and countries are still trying to one up each other. I think that's why I must have become a cosmonaut; to get away from all the bullshit on Earth. Well, that, and trying to get closer to my illustrious father. If I hadn't joined the corps I probably would only have ever seen him at Christmas. Maybe that would have been better."

Hopper nodded understandingly. "The world needs men like your father, but when they come along it's their families who suffer. The future never stops arriving, Lexi. Tomorrow is always just out of reach, and as long as that's true, there's always the chance that things will get better."

"There won't be a tomorrow if the League of Joa release the virus back home."

"We won't let that happen, Lexi. We'll warn everybody. They'll find a way to fight it if it ever happens."

She smiled mirthlessly. "Wish I could be the unflappable hero like you. Were you the same way when you took down that Russian Destroyer all by yourself?"

Hopper looked away and down at the floor. "I never took down that Destroyer. It surrendered."

"What?"

"The Russians on board were defectors. They wanted to give themselves up but were afraid of their own Government. They wanted asylum. I was only there to communicate with them, non-threateningly in my little Warrior, and take their demands. They asked for the British or American Space Corps to take them into custody, but we refused. I was there to track them, make sure they didn't disappear. They never fired on me once and I never fired on them. Eventually they were so desperate that they begged me to turn back and just let them flee, but I refused. I was young and naïve, eager to impress my superiors. I believed that the Russian

Government would deal with its defectors humanely, but when the convoy arrived it stormed the Destroyer and killed every last man on board. I watched their corpses jettison into space."

Lexi blinked slowly. "Why did the Russian men surrender to their Government if they were so afraid?"

"Because when the Russian convoy arrived, it was accompanied by a British ambassador. Our man assured the defectors that they would be treated well and that Britain would oversee their sentencing and ensure their rights were maintained. It was a lie – a favour to the Russian President. The Russian Space Navy was welcomed aboard with open arms, but they slaughtered every last man. To ensure my silence, SABA covered me in medals and made me the most senior pilot in the corps with a heroic story to match. My entire career rests on a foundation of blood. Nothing I ever do will change that."

"Why did you agree to keep it secret?" Lexi wasn't judging, just curious to see why a man as unflappable as Hopper had not done the right thing.

"It was made very clear to me that I either took a medal for living courageously or a bullet for living carelessly. They made me piss my pants like some green recruit, Lexi. From that day forward I made sure I was the best damn pilot SABA had. If I became an institution, like you father, then they would have no threat great enough to cow me. If they ever tried to force my silence again, I would expose their secrets, and people would listen because I'm the most decorated pilot in the corps. I protected myself by being the best. Maybe they sent me here to get rid of me. Maybe SABA knew what we were walking into."

Lexi shook her head. "My father would never have brought me here if he had any idea."

"I suppose you're right. Still, I don't intend on dying up here.

I'm going to make it back to Earth so I can finally be the thorn in SABA's side that I always should have been. I used to think that those Russian defectors died because of me, but after seeing what's happened here, I've realised that the people controlling who lives and who dies are wearing ties and sitting behind large desks. Perhaps it's always been that way."

Lexi nodded. "But as long as there's a tomorrow, there's a chance it might not always be that way."

"Hell, yes."

Lexi finished her coffee and stood up. "Let's go home."

They decided not to set off back through the Ice Lands, for they knew for sure that there were dead people somewhere within the amusement park, including the large pack that had swarmed Miller. They chose to travel from the base of the Astronomer's Finger into the hotel and recreational grounds of Grand Galaxy. The first place they entered was a garden area outside of a spa and swimming pool facility. They stayed outside the buildings and kept to the gardens. The well-cultivated lawns and plants made it almost feel as if they were back on Earth. The ceiling overhead even had a blue sky projected onto it with fluffy white clouds drifting across it.

There were no obstacles as they passed through the garden and Lexi even felt herself begin to relax, which was probably the whole point. By the time they left the area and entered into the courtyard of one of the park's hotels, they were unprepared for danger, which was why Hopper was caught off completely off guard.

The bellhop leapt out from behind a pillar and fell on top of Hopper. Hopper was caught mid-stride and tripped over his own legs, tumbling onto his side. The bellhop would have taken a bite out of him if not for the fact Lexi wrapped an arm around his neck and pulled him away. She fought to hold the dead man still while Hopper climbed back to his feet and aimed his pistol.

"Get clear," he shouted.

Lexi shoved the bellhop in the back and sidestepped out of the way. Hopper lined up his shot and placed a round right through the bellhop's eye. The gun's report wasn't particularly loud, about the same as a door slamming, but it was enough to encourage movement from inside the hotel.

Lexi was the first to notice. Inside the glass-fronted lobby of the hotel, several bodies appeared. Followed by dozens more. Before long there were a hundred of more guests gathered inside the lobby, and all of them were dead.

Hopper stepped over the bellhop and pointed his pistol again, but he lowered it when he realised his intention of shooting them was farcical.

Bodies continued appearing in the lobby and the entire mob began moving towards the courtyard.

"There must be a thousand people crammed inside there," Hopper said, overestimating a little but not by much.

"That's where all the guests have been this whole time. They're all packed up inside the hotels."

Hopper was already walking backwards, poised to turn around and run. "When the shit hit the fan, people must have made for their rooms. Maybe security even called for the guests to do so. They must have been slaughtered like cattle."

The first bodies pushed through the entryway and moved out into the courtyard. When they set eyes on Lexi and Hopper, they picked up speed.

Neither of them bothered to shout, Run, for they both knew the drill well enough by now. They fled the courtyard and moved into another garden area. When they reached the end of it and neared the next hotel courtyard, they were faced with yet another mob. The noise of the gunshot had travelled.

"We're screwed," Lexi said.

Hopper started letting off shots, taking down a few bodies, but it was a drop in the ocean. His gun soon ran dry and Lexi knocked it out of his hand. "That shooting will have just attracted even more."

"Shit, I'm sorry."

"Don't be sorry, just be fast."

They ran for their lives, dodging between probing hands and chattering teeth. At one point, Lexi fell into the grasp of a skinny woman in broken heels, but Hopper leapt up and kicked her away. Luckily, the woman's heels were such a mess that she tottered over and let go of Lexi.

They carried on through the crowd, picking up an entourage of the dead as they tried to find safety. If the courtyard were any more cramped, they would be done for, but luckily it was a large open area and the dead tended to bunch together in small groups. For the time being there was still opportunity to cut a path.

Eventually the way ahead became blocked. There were just too many bodies now to navigate through, and a parked people mover lay right in their escape path.

Lexi ran into the people mover and put her back against it. The clean white electric vehicle had a small driver's compartment at the front and an affixed carriage with four rows of benches at the back. Dead men and women closed in on all sides.

"There's no escape," Lexi said.

"Nope," Hopper agreed.

A woman made a grab for Lexi and reflexively she grabbed the driver compartment's door and swung it open by the handle. The aluminium edge struck the women in the face and opened up the flesh from her left eye all the way down to her chin. Opening the door also did something else; it presented an option.

Hopper jumped inside the compartment and dragged Lexi in backwards after him. Understanding, she hooked the door with her foot and pulled it closed again.

Dead hands and teeth battered the windows immediately.

Hopper grabbed Lexi and pulled her up into a sitting position. "Are you okay?" he said. "Did any of them get you?"

"I don't know." She patted herself down. "No, I don't think so."

"Good, because I don't drive with no zombie woman." He pulled out the zipline from his comms unit and inserted it into the dashboard. Suddenly the cabin came to life with a dozen blinking lights.

Lexi smiled. At least Hopper was still thinking clearly. She would have sat in the cabin and wept, completely forgetting that the people movers at Grand Galaxies had computers that could be accessed and overridden.

Hopper pulled the lever and put the vehicle into drive. There were several bodies in front of them, trying to bust in through the windscreen, but by keeping their speed slow, Hopper was able to gradually shunt them out of the way. Once clear, he pulled the lever again and picked up speed. But it appeared that top speed was not much faster than a brisk jog. While it got them away from the murderous mob, the faster of their pursuers were able to keep up and even run alongside the vehicle.

"I can pee faster than this," Hopper said, growling.

"Just keep going. At least it's bought us some breathing space. Most of them are falling back."

They made it onto a wide paved area that seemed to be for both pedestrians and people movers, for it contained both benches and abandoned people movers. Some of the pursuing dead people collided with the benches as they ran and fell to the ground, but there were still several dozen still giving chase.

A sign at the side of the road announced: TRANSPORTATION CENTRE.

"Head for that," Lexi shouted.

"I hear you." It would have been a good time to pick up speed, but as they were already maxed out, Hopper just kept them on the road and followed the correct path when the way forward split in two. The road ahead narrowed and was lined on either side by two grassy banks. It had the added bonus of corralling the pursuing dead and reducing their speed as a whole. Lexi and Hopper began to gain a little distance.

Ahead, the road split again. They had the option of continuing to the Transportation Centre, or heading right towards NEW ARRIVALS. Hopper took the right path, knowing where it would lead them.

"We're almost back to the Hermes," Lexi said. "We've almost made it."

Hopper gritted his teeth and said, "You can rely on Space Hopper Airways to cover all your travelling needs."

Lexi chuckled. She was almost giddy at the thought of reaching the terminal and getting back into the Hermes. Once they were back inside that cockpit, there would be no stopping them from making it back home.

But getting to the Hermes was not going to be as easy as they hoped. When they reached the terminal, someone was there waiting for them. Cog.

-15-

Hopper narrowed his eyes. "Cog!"

He slammed on the brake and brought the people mover to a stop in the middle of the road. The way it sat, slightly at an angle, meant that it blocked the entrance and would prevent the dead from getting through into the terminal. Lexi wondered if he did it on purpose. Even if he did, it wasn't going to matter very much, for Cog was perfectly capable of killing them on his own.

Or not exactly on his own.

Standing with Cog was a line of humanoids, five in total. They stood to attention, somehow under his command.

"Get out of there," Cog shouted at them. He still had the revolver from earlier and was pointing it right at them.

Lexi looked at Hopper. Hopper looked at Lexi.

"What should we do?" Lexi asked.

"I guess we do as the lovely man tells us."

Lexi swallowed and then opened her door. She could hear and feel the banging from the rear of the people mover, and as she looked back she could see over the benches that there was a mob of dead people trying to get past the obstacle in their way.

"Come closer," Cog said. "I want to talk to you."

Lexi frowned, but did as she was asked. Both she and Hopper

walked over until Cog stopped them about eight feet away. From this close the diseased man was disgusting and smelt absolutely foul. Lexi eyed his robotic companions cautiously.

"Don't worry about them," Cog said in a slur. Drool escaped his swollen black lips as he spoke and one of his eyes was dead and unmoving. "They been behaving very strangely since you brought them back online, but I assure you I have these ones under very strict control."

"How?" Hopper asked. "Weren't you just a warehouse monkey?"

If the comment annoyed Cog, it did not show, for his face was now covered in the little black tendrils of his diseased veins. No expression came to his face except one of suffering.

"I was a team leader, but that is besides the point. I took the comms unit from your dead soldier left in the canyon."

Lexi groaned. "Miller."

"Yes, well. I took his comms unit and was quite delighted to find that it contained overrides for...well, just about everything. Allowed me to hack into my humanoid friends and have them follow me. Good thing, too, because you can't possibly leave."

"Screw you," Hopper said. "We're getting out of here."

Cog shook his head. A wound opened up in the crease of his neck and begun bleeding. "Don't you understand? Surely, now, you must. This disease can't make it back to Earth. It has to die here, with us."

"We're not infected," Lexi said.

"No way to be sure. It's too much of a risk. It could be on your clothes, you hair – anywhere. You might be carriers. I admit to not knowing much about diseases, but I know it's too much of a risk for anybody to leave here. The security team understood that. I saw them massacre hundreds of guests trying to contact home. Communications were shut off pretty quickly after that."

"You mean the jamming wasn't you?" Hopper said.

"No. The security team understood the need to contain things. I overheard them talking about what this place really is – the secrets contained here. Once the disease reached here, it was only ever going to end one way. When they cut the power to the terminal, shortly after you arrived, I grabbed a radio and tried to warn you that there was no leaving here. Still, you gave things a good go. I expect a team from Earth will come and put a torch to this place soon."

"My father is destroying it," Lexi said. "He's going to turn the orbital lasers inwards and destroy the facility."

Cog let out a sigh that sounded very much like relief. "That is...very good to hear."

"Why do you want to see everyone dead so badly?" Hopper said. "Are you really that worried about Earth? You think you're some kind of martyr?"

"I have an ex-wife and two children back on Earth. I may not have been the greatest father, but I love my family. I would rather die for certain than take the smallest risk that they might instead. This disease started with me the moment I opened that blasted crate, but I will make sure my children never have to suffer the way I have."

"We can get you help," Lexi said. "You're different to the others. There may be a way."

"I'll be dead within the hour," he said. "I can feel my body shutting down. I can barely breathe. I have just long enough to see things through. You say your father is going to blow this place up? When?"

"When we leave," Lexi said. "If you keep us here, he won't do it."

"Well, that's a shame. I suppose I will just have to deal with you myself and hope that the clean-up team does their job. I can't see that they won't. They'll probably nuke this entire place."

"You don't know what you're talking about," Hopper said. "We came here to help, not destroy."

"Funny then, how one of you has their finger on a button somewhere, ready to blow this place up. Are you really trying to tell me that your mission wasn't to contain this however necessary?"

Hopper glanced at Lexi and she could tell he was thinking about what her father had told them. The mission always had been to contain the situation, however necessary.

"Just let us go," Lexi almost begged.

"I'm afraid I can't. Humanoid units, I command you to use lethal force against these two criminals."

The five humanoids all looked up as one, their blue eyes glaring into Lexi and Hopper. "You have been condemned by Grand Galaxy Amusement Park Management. Surrender now or lethal force will be used against you."

"I'm really starting to hate these things," Hopper said.

Lexi took a step back. "Don't blame the computer, blame the operator."

They were completely unarmed; fighting the humanoids would be suicide. Lexi started moving away and had to grab Hopper to get him going with her. The humanoids stalked towards them slowly, their design too primitive to allow them to run. It was the only advantage they had. Lexi headed towards one of the reception desks, hoping to place a barrier between her and the machines hunting her. But before she got there a shot rang out and something stung her. The pain radiated throughout her legs and back and sent her sprawling into the area behind the reception desk.

Hopper saw she was hit and ran over to her. He rolled her onto her side and ran his hands all over her. "Damn it."

"What?" Lexi said, fighting the urge to vomit. "Where am I hit?"

Hopper shook his head. "The sonofabitch shot you in the ass."

Lexi groaned. She was in so much pain.

"SURRENDER NOW OR FACE LETHAL CONSEQUENCES."

Over the din of his humanoids, Cog shouted a final warning. "Give yourselves up and we can sit it out together. You're not leaving here, but you can still have a final few hours of peace."

"The only peace I'm going to be having is out of your ass," Hopper said. He turned to Lexi and sighed. "That sounded really wrong, didn't it?"

Lexi shivered with pain, but managed to say, "I think he got the point."

One of the humanoids made it around the desk and spotted Lexi and Hopper hiding.

Hopper put his head under Lexi's arm and pulled her to her feet. As soon as their heads went above the desk, another shot rang out from Cog's revolver. It went wide.

Hopper and Lexi crouched down and moved away just as the Humanoid snatched at them. The rest of the humanoids were nearby and approached the desk. Lexi was numb from the waist down. Every step she took was clumsy and Hopper was obviously struggling to keep hold of her.

"SURRENDER NOW."

Hopper snarled. "Bite me, you overgrown food blender."

Lexi saw Cog lining up another shot and yanked Hopper down. "Duck."

The shot hit a sign placed on the wall behind the desk.

"We're surrounded," Hopper said, finally sounding desperate.

"I have an idea," Lexi said. "The people mover."

"You want to drive out of here?"

"Something like that."

"There's no way we can make it back to the people mover," Hopper said.

Lexi nodded. "I know. That's why I'm going to distract cog while you go."

Hopper was confused, but when she quickly explained her plan, he nodded and said, "Okay, it just might work."

"Then get moving." Lexi shoved Hopper away and threw herself out from behind the desk. The numbness in her legs was now complete and she tumbled to her knees, but kept her hands in the air. "Okay, okay, I surrender."

The humanoids stopped coming towards her.

"REMAIN STILL. A MEMBER OF SECURITY WILL COME TO ARREST YOU SHORTLY."

Cog took a cautious step towards her, keeping his revolver pointed at her face. "Where's your boyfriend?"

"Still hiding behind the desk," she lied. Hopefully Hopper had already snuck around the back and started heading towards the people mover.

"Either you both surrender or no deal. Your partner has ten seconds to come out and join you or I put a bullet between those lovely eyes of yours. DO YOU HEAR ME? COME OUT OR I SHOOT YOUR PRETTY LADY."

Hopper didn't come out. Good, Lexi thought. If you surrender then this whole thing is finished. We'll never get out of here. Stick to the plan, Hopper.

"Come out now," Cog snarled. "I am not a lenient man."

"Okay, okay. I'm coming." Hopper's voice was far off. He had managed to sneak away.

Cog's swollen eyes narrowed. "What are you doing over there?"

There was a soft whirring of an electric motor and that was Lexi's cue. She willed her numb legs to wake up for just as second and threw herself at Cog. She had six feet to cover, but his attention was taken up trying to discover where Hopper was and what was making the noise. By the time he spotted Lexi, and tried to turn his gun on her, she was tackling him to the ground and landing a punch in the centre of his face. The black veins ruptured and his skin peeled away, revealing blackened tissue and weeping pus underneath. Her knuckles were caked in gore, which she quickly wiped on his overalls.

She was about to climb to her feet when something crushed down on her shoulder and yanked her up painfully. "YOU HAVE COMMITTED ASSAULT. YOU ARE UNDER ARREST. LETHAL FORCE HAS BEEN AUTHORISED."

Lexi felt the pressure on her shoulder increase as the humanoid squeezed harder. She cried out in agony.

"YOU HAVE FAILED TO SURRENDER. LETHAL FORCE INITIATED."

Lexi's eyes rolled back in her head as the pain dragged her towards unconsciousness.

Suddenly the pressure released, but before it did, the hand around Lexi's shoulder pulled her to the ground. She gasped and then wailed, every muscle in her body aching. The humanoid hit the floor and slid a dozen feet across the floor on its back. Something had struck it hard.

Hopper pulled the people mover to a halt right beside Lexi and flung open the passenger door. "Get in!"

Lexi couldn't get to her feet so she crawled, reached up for Hopper's hand, and then dragged herself up into the cabin. She couldn't get the door closed fast enough and a humanoid appeared and grabbed her by the arm. It started to pull her right back out again. Hopper grabbed her other arm and tried to keep her inside. He couldn't hope to match the strength of a machine, though.

Lexi was halfway back out the cabin when somebody came to her aid. The man was middle-aged with thinning, receding hair. One of his eyes was missing and his lower jaw hung at an unnatural angle. The dead man didn't intentionally come to her rescue; in fact it wanted to get at her, but the humanoid took it as an offensive action and released Lexi in order to grab the dead man by both shoulders. As it began to squeeze, the sound of the dead man's collarbones snapping echoed off the glass dome above their heads.

Lexi pulled herself back inside the cabin and slammed the door closed. Hopper pulled the lever and got them moving.

The humanoids now were surrounded by the dead and sought to arrest each and every one of them. They did not understand that the former guests were no longer human. "YOU ARE UNDER ARREST," they squawked, but the dead did not listen.

"Look out," Lexi said.

Cog stood in their path, his ruined face discernable only by the bulging red eyes. He raised his revolver but did not fire. When he turned the weapon to inspect it, it was clear that he had run out of ammunition.

Hopper stared ahead with grim determination, but he had one last comment to make before they headed down the gantry towards the Hermes. "Nothing like a vacation to make you realise how much you love home."

The people mover smashed into Cog hard enough that his virus-ridden body tore apart. One of his arms came loose and went up the windscreen, but the rest of him went under the big rubber tyres and came out the back as a sticky black puddle.

-16-

Several dead guests broke off from the crowd and followed the people mover into the tunnel. Like before, it was only the fastest that could keep up.

Hopper slammed on the brakes and turned the vehicle sideways, blocking off the corridor like he had the road into the terminal earlier. Then he leapt out. Lexi dragged herself across the seat and went out the same way, as the dead guests were coming up on her side.

A dead man threw himself across one of the benches of the passenger section of the people mover and started climbing out the other side. Lexi hobbled over to him and started punching him in the head.

"Leave it," Hopper said. "We need to make it to the Hermes."

Lexi realised he was right. She couldn't fight the dead with her fists alone. She gritted her teeth and followed after Hopper, who wasn't much faster. Both of them were done physically, neither having anything left in the tank. They reached the end of the gantry and Hopper collapsed against the wall beside the airlock control panel. He pulled the zipline from his comm unit and accessed the door controls.

Lexi stood anxiously, watching the dead guests climb their

way over the benches of the people mover. The man she had punched was already through and was now hurrying towards them. "Hey, Hopper, you want to hurry it up?"

"I'm just synching up. One second."

"You have half-a-second."

The dead man was on them. It reached out for Lexi, teeth gnashing in anticipation of biting her. Lexi pressed her back against the wall, too weak to put up a fight. The wall suddenly disappeared and she was staggering backwards. Hopper caught her and the two of them stumbled inside the Hermes. As they entered, the interior lights switched on. The systems were back online.

The dead man made it inside, too, but Hopper had enough energy left to boot the man in the stomach and send him back out. Then he bashed the airlock control button and the door began to slide back down again. The dead man tried to get inside but the door came down on top of him and cut him in two. The airlock closed. They were safe.

Lexi and Hopper both collapsed at the same time onto the cabin's passenger bench. Lexi moaned while Hopper panted.

"W-we made it," she said, wincing and rubbing herself in a dozen places.

Hopper leaned forward on his knees and let his head hang. "I'm too old for thrill rides."

Lexi looked down at the top half of the body trapped in the airlock. We can't leave that there."

"We'll put it in the hold. It's airtight. We can warn them when we land."

They took a five-minute breather and then got up. They grabbed the dismembered torso by each arm and lifted it easily, surprised by how much lighter a body was without its legs and waist. There was also a lack of blood; just a concealed mess from a system that no longer worked, a heart that no longer pumped. There was a sticky mess beneath the airlock door, but there was little they could do about it until they landed. They could request quarantine procedure and a HAZMAT team would hose down the entire craft.

They shoved the body into the airtight lockers at the rear of the cabin. They were designed to hold food and supplies on longer trips, but they would do just as well as quarantine containers. Hopper slammed down the lid and engaged the lock. "Let's get out of her," he said.

"Lexi, is that you?"

Lexi spun around, her heart leaping into her mouth. Her father's voice.

"The radio," Hopper said, pointing. The cockpit was lit up again, working as normal.

Lexi went over and flipped the switch to open communications. "Dad, is that you? Are comms back online?"

"No, they're still down. I'm on the dead captain's radio. Short wave still works since Hopper removed the jamming signal. I'm still in the comms suite. When you engaged the airlock it came up on my screen. Are you alright?"

"Yes, dad. I'm...alive. Hopper is still with me. We're about to disengage and get out of here."

"Good. You have no idea how much it means knowing you're going to get out of here alive."

Lexi reached out a hand and touched the radio unit, wishing it were her father and not just his voice. "Are you still going through with it?"

"Nothing's changed. If they send a clean up crew here, there's a chance the virus may make it back to Earth. Other nations will try to interfere, demanding to know what happened to the guests.

It's too much of a risk. I have everything set. Just get out of here."

"Dad…I'm going to miss you."

There was a brief silence, followed by, "I could have been a better father, Lexi, I know that. But I'm proud of you. Commander Sharman – dad – over and out."

The radio crackled and went silent.

Lexi tried to get her father back but it was no use. He was gone.

Hopper placed a hand on her shoulder and made her wince. The muscle there had been reduced to mush. "Sorry," he said. "We need to go."

Lexi nodded and went and took her seat in the navigator's chair while Hopper took up the flight seat. He ran through the pre-flight checks as quickly as was safe to, then ran the disengagement protocols.

There was the obligatory loud clunking as metal parts shifted and uncoupled, followed by the Hermes' thrusters igniting. Then they were away, floating sideways away from the airlock and into space. Hooper kicked the thrusters into gear and they took off, fast enough to force Lexi back in her chair.

"Sorry," Hopper told her. "My nerves are a little shot."

"I'm sure you're still the best pilot in the corps."

"Damn straight."

Once they were safely away, Hopper dropped their speed to something a little more comfortable. Lexi stared out of the cockpit window at Grand Galaxies and no longer saw an impressive feat of human engineering but a place of horror and nightmares. Mankind's relentless efforts to exceed itself would one day bring about its ruin, she was sure of it. The closer they came to being gods, the closer they came to extinction.

"Would you buy a return ticket?" Hopper asked her as they passed by the Astronomer's Finger. Lexi tried to see her father somewhere near the top, by the giant satellite dish, but it was impossible. She shook her head. "Not a chance. I hope my father manages to wipe this monstrosity off the surface of the moon."

"I think he's about to. Look!"

Lexi looked out the window and saw a huge expanse of the moon's surface opening up. From beneath the crust a platform began to rise. On the platform was a cannon twice as long as the Astronomer's Finger. She also noticed that sheets of metal, moved into place to stop the guests ever seeing the true purpose of Installation 23, now covered the glass sides of the Finger tower, making it look like a giant bullet.

Slowly the cannon began to swivel on its base. At the same time it changed its aim from directly upwards to more horizontal. Eventually it aimed directly at Grand Galaxies.

"Time to get out of here," Hopper said. "Hold on."

Lexi gripper her armrests and leant back into her seat as Hopper kicked the thrusters into overdrive and whipped them away from the surface of the moon. The windows filled with only the blackness of space and the twinkling of distant stars. Then the entire cockpit filled with light and they began spinning and vibrating. Alarms went off, warning them that control had been lost. Lexi grabbed her control panel, priming the stabilising thrusters, but before she managed to activate them, Hopper held the ship steady and got them back on course. A couple of minutes later, he banked to the left and gave them a view of what they were leaving behind.

The moon had a new crater.

#

It was about ninety minutes later, almost halfway between the moon and the earth when somebody hailed them on a restricted channel.

Hopper gave Lexi an anxious look then answered the call. "SABA vessel 416-19. Authorisation code: Hotel-Lima-Tango-One. Flight Master Hopper."

"Master Hopper? Is that really you, sir? Wow, it's an honour."

Hopper sighed loudly and gave Lexi a smile. They could both tell from the clear British accent that they had SABA on the line.

"Yes, it really is me. I have Lieutenant Sharman with me. We're the only two survivors returning from aborted an mission to secure Facility 23."

"I'm aware of the mission, Master Hopper. Please report."

"The facility is gone. Commander Sharman turned the weapon systems in on themselves and levelled the entire area. All assets lost."

There was a clearing of a throat, followed by, "Weapons systems?"

Hopper sighed. "Probably above your pay grade, my friend. Requesting safe landing at London Terminal. Quarantine procedures advised."

"Negative. Flagship Destroyer Kestral is in your sector. They will take you in and conduct quarantine protocols there and receive immediate debriefing."

"Copy that."

Lexi was relieved. The blood under the airlock door worried her and she was glad that quarantine would take place on a Destroyer faraway from Earth. She knew the Kestrel well, had flown many sorties based out of there. Its commander, Johnson, had been a friend of her father's. He father had had a lot of friends.

Hopper brought the Hermes to a holding position and they waited for a little over twenty minutes until a small grey speck appeared before them. Gradually that speck grew into a hulking great monolith that filled their entire view.

Hopper whistled. "I'll be glad to take a shower when all this is over. I can't believe we actually made it out of this alive."

"Me either," Lexi said. "It still all seems like a nightmare, you know?"

"That's because it was a nightmare."

Hopper handed over the controls to the Kestrel who remote controlled the Hermes into an airlock and fixed them in place. It took a little over five minutes for the entire procedure to complete.

The radio hissed. "Stand by Master Hopper. A team will be with you shortly."

"Copy that."

Hopper eased up out of his seat and went over and helped Lexi out of hers. Together they made a sorry sight, holding one another up and wincing with the slightest movement. They made their way over to the airlock door and waited to be taken care of.

A few minutes later, the airlock clunked and then began to open, rising slowly from the floor. The first thing they saw were the dark black boots of the welcome party. Then they saw the rifles pointing at them.

Lexi was too confused to say anything, but she heard Hopper mutter to himself one word, "Shit!"

The welcome team opened fire.

-Epilogue-

Squad leader Tanner was the one to put a bullet in the wheezing pilot, a burden he was willing to take for his men. It was a shame killing a man as decorated as Flight Master Hopper, and Commander Sharman's daughter, no less, but Commander Johnson's orders had been explicit. There were sensitive secrets inside the heads of the two cosmonauts aboard the Hermes and they needed eliminating for the sake of Allied Security. Tanner couldn't imagine what, exactly, they had come across on the surface of the moon, but he knew better than to ask. There was always a bigger picture when it came to SABA's motives and he only had to believe that the greater good was at stake. Just a pity that Facility 23 had needed to be destroyed. His kids loved Grand Galaxies.

His corporal came up to report. "There's nobody else on board, sir. The forensic team is arriving to investigate the mess beneath the airlock. The pilot requested quarantine protocols before he docked so Commander Johnson is concerned that a biological attack may have caused the communications blackout at Facility 23."

Tanner nodded. "Whatever it was, led to them wiping Grand Galaxies off the moon, so it wouldn't surprise me if it was something biological. Make sure you and the other men take a chemical shower before leaving the docking bay."

"Copy that." The corporal turned on his heel and scuttled away.

Tanner remained alone inside the cabin of the Hermes, surveying the mess. The two cosmonauts now lay side by side on the passenger benches and would soon be taken away. Flight Master Hopper had a bullet hole right between his eyes where Tanner had finished him and he congratulated himself for such a good shot. With so many good men and woman gone due to the disastrous mission to the moon, there would now be several positions opening up in the corp. Maybe he could apply for Lieutenant Sharman's rank. Her daddy couldn't do anyone any favours anymore.

While he waited to hand over to the incoming forensics team, Tanner looked around for anything of interest – anything that might bring him even more favour with Commander Johnson. The best place to look was the cargo hold at the rear of the small craft. Anything pertaining to the mission would lay in there.

He moved over to the lockers and turned the dial, unlocking the seal and loosening the lid. When he did so, there was a clunking sound that made him think something was inside. He pulled up the lid to take a look and something leapt out at him, clamping down on his arm.

"What the fuck!"

A dismembered torso dragged itself out of the cargo locker, tearing into Tanner's wrist with its teeth. He managed to shake the man free and throw the torso to the floor where it immediately started grasping for his leg. He took a step back and pulled his sidearm from its holster. He fired off three rounds, two into the monster's back and a final one in the top of its skull.

The gruesome thing stopped moving and Tanner stepped away breathlessly. His arm was throbbing and bleeding where teeth had torn his flesh. It throbbed terribly. He wiped away the blood with his hand and rolled down his sleeve; didn't want his men to know he had taken a wound.

The forensic team entered, wearing their HAZMAT suits, but also carrying pistols. It was unusual for forensics to be armed.

"Squad Leader Tanner, is the area secure?"

Tanner looked down at the bleeding torso and almost said no, but he had a feeling that admitting so would be a mistake. "Everything is secure," he said. Two dead and...and half a body in the cargo lockers." He pointed to the torso.

"Did you get any blood on you?"

"What?"

"Squad Leader Tanner, did you get any blood on you from either of the passengers or the dead man at your feet?"

"Er, no, no. The passengers were shot from distance and I used my glove to pull this body out onto the floor."

"Make sure you burn your gloves, Squad Leader Tanner. Dismissed."

Tanner swallowed a lump in his throat and nodded. As he walked away, he decided it would be a bad idea to tell the ship's doctors that he'd taken a bite on his arm. Maybe when he got back to Earth he would get it checked out, but no way was he telling anybody about it now. Something was going on that he didn't want to know about. He quickly forgot about promotions and decided to keep his head down. He buttoned his cuff and decided to wear long sleeve shirts until he made it back to Earth. The bite mark continued to throb.

END

About The Author

Iain Rob Wright is one of the UK's most successful horror and suspense writers, with novels including the critically acclaimed, THE FINAL WINTER; the disturbing bestseller, ASBO; and the wicked screamfest, THE HOUSEMATES.

His work is currently being adapted for graphic novels, audio books, and foreign audiences. He is an active member of the Horror Writer Association and a massive animal lover.

Check out Iain's official website or add him on Facebook where he would love to meet you.

www.iainrobwright.com

FEAR ON EVERY PAGE

Printed in Great Britain
by Amazon